The Mystery of Death Trap Mine

D1353461

Alfred Hitchcock and
The Three Investigators

in

The Mystery of
Death Trap Mine

Text by M. V. Carey

Based on characters created by Robert Arthur

Armada

First published in the U.K. in 1977 by
William Collins Sons & Co. Ltd., London and Glasgow.
This edition was first published in Armada in 1980 by
Fontana Paperbacks,
14 St. James's Place, London SW1A 1PS.

Printed in Great Britain by
Love & Malcomson Ltd., Brighton Road,
Redhill, Surrey.

Contents

A Word
from Alfred Hitchcock

Greetings, mystery lovers!

Once more I invite you to share in the exploits of The Three Investigators—that trio of adventurous young detectives who specialize in solving mysteries of an unusual, if not bizarre, nature. I hope that those of you who are brave of heart will relish a journey with them to a remote New Mexico mining town where a dead man waits in a dead mine to betray a living scoundrel . . . and where a mysterious woman—but I am getting ahead of myself!

If by chance you are not already acquainted with The Three Investigators, let me state that Jupiter Jones, leader of the group, is a plump lad with an excellent memory and an astounding talent for deduction. Pete Crenshaw is quick and athletic, but in his more cautious moments is apt to deplore Jupiter's penchant for stirring up trouble. Bob Andrews is a studious fellow who is in charge of research and records for the trio. The lads reside in Rocky Beach, California, on the outskirts of Los Angeles, but they are never averse to travelling far afield in search of mystery and intrigue.

So much for the formalities. You may now turn immediately to chapter one and get on with the story.

ALFRED HITCHCOCK

I

The Invitation

"HEY, JUPE! Guess who's looking for you!" said Pete Crenshaw as he pushed open a trap-door in the floor and scrambled into the Headquarters of The Three Investigators.

"I don't need to guess. I know," said Jupiter Jones. He leaned back in his chair, which squeaked under the weight of his chubby frame. "Aunt Mathilda was up at six o'clock this morning," he said, in his precise way. "She cooked a hearty breakfast and sent Uncle Titus off to a garage sale in Oxnard. I deduced at once that she planned a busy day." Jupiter peered at his watch. "It is now exactly one-fifteen. From your question, I now deduce that Uncle Titus has returned, that he has made some purchases in Oxnard, and that Aunt Mathilda wishes me to help unload the truck."

"Jupiter Jones, boy genius!" Bob Andrews chuckled. The slender, bespectacled youth was leaning on a filing cabinet, quietly reading through some notes.

The three boys were in the battered old mobile home trailer that Jupe's aunt and uncle had given them for a clubhouse. It sat in a far corner of The

Jones Salvage Yard, concealed behind stacks of old timber, beams, and scrap iron. The salvage yard was a busy place. Filled with all sorts of ordinary scrap, it also contained a variety of unusual items rescued from houses that were being torn down—antique sundials, old marble bathtubs, carved door-frames, and stained-glass windows. As they were always busy cleaning, sorting, and storing these things—and waiting on people who came from up and down the Pacific Coast looking for hard-to-find objects—Jupiter's uncle and aunt had completely forgotten about the trailer in the corner.

The boys had turned the trailer into a head-quarters for their junior detective firm—The Three Investigators. Inside was a tiny lab and darkroom, and an office fitted out with a worn desk, chairs, and a telephone. A large filing cabinet held reports on all the boys' cases, meti-culously written up by Bob Andrews. Jupiter, the leader of the trio, spent much of his free time in Headquarters, pondering the firm's cases and exercising his incredible brain.

Jupiter was proud of his uncanny knack for deduction. Now, as Pete and Bob grinned at him, he scowled. "Aunt Mathilda is *not* looking for me?" he asked.

"Don't complain," said Pete. "When Aunt Mathilda's looking for you, you know what it means—work! No. 1 was down at the Rocky Beach Market this morning and I bumped into Allie Jamison."

Jupe sat suddenly upright in his chair. Bob

stopped shuffling papers and stared. Allie Jamison, the daughter of one of the wealthiest families in Rocky Beach, had been their client the summer before. In a case they called *The Mystery of the Singing Serpent*, they had helped her get rid of a sinister house-guest and had exposed a diabolical blackmail plot. But their association with the girl had not been a complete pleasure. She was impulsive, devoted to getting her own way, and not above bending the truth when it suited her.

"Oh, good grief!" said Jupe at last. "I thought that girl was spending the summer with an uncle in New Mexico. The Jamison house is closed up and Mr and Mrs Jamison are in Japan!"

Pete nodded. "I know. But right now Allie is here in Rocky Beach. She told me she and her uncle needed to pick up some stuff from the house, and her uncle had business in town. And something's up with her. She's just busting with some great news and she's going to come tell us about it before she and her uncle leave for New Mexico."

Bob sighed. "And it started out to be such a peaceful summer."

"Never mind," said Jupiter. "She *is* leaving again—soon, one hopes! Pete, how long will Allie be here?"

"Only until tomorrow!" said a voice from behind the curtain that separated the little laboratory section of the trailer from the office. Pete groaned as the curtain was pulled to one side and Allie Jamison stepped out, grinning. She looked like a young rodeo rider in her faded jeans and western shirt. Her face was tanned and her long, tawny hair was sun-streaked. "Aren't you glad to see me?" she asked innocently. But her hazel eyes sparkled with malicious glee.

"How did you get in here?" demanded Pete.

Allie laughed. She went to the desk, pulled herself up on to it, and sat there cross-legged. "I got here ahead of all of you," she said. "There's a painting of the great San Francisco fire on the back fence of this place, and in the painting there's a little dog watching the fire."

Jupe slouched wearily. "And there's a knothole in the dog's eye. You stuck your finger through the knothole, undid a catch on the inside of the fence, and the boards swung open." Jupiter was referring to Red Gate Rover, one of several secret entrances to the salvage yard that the boys had devised.

"You deduced right this time," said Allie. "I watched you guys open that gate at least a dozen times last summer. And I didn't have to be an Einstein to figure out that you had some kind of secret hideout back here."

"Go ahead, Allie," said Pete. "Rub it in. How did you get in here?"

Allie went on with obvious delight. "You guys aren't as smart as you think! There's a sign that says 'Office' on top of a pile of junk right inside that gate. But the arrow on the sign doesn't point to the junkyard office. So I figured it must point to your detective headquarters, And I was right! I just followed the arrow through the junk . . . and ended up in front of that sliding panel." Allie pointed to a panel at the back of the trailer. "That's darn good detective work, if I do say so myself," said Allie.

"We must put a lock on that panel," said Jupe.

"Yeah, and take down that sign!" added Pete.

"Don't bother," snapped Allie. "I *am* leaving tomorrow, and I don't care about your silly secrets anyway." She gave a saucy toss of her head. "Besides, I've got better things to do."

"Such as what?" demanded Pete.

Allie leaned forward intently. "I've got a case of my own," she said. "I'm going to investigate like you guys, and I'm going to keep my Uncle Harry from having the wool pulled over his eyes."

"Oh?" said Jupe. "Is your Uncle Harry incapable of taking care of himself?"

Allie's face was serious. "My Uncle Harry is Harrison Osborne, and he's no dope," she told them. "He made a couple of fortunes in the stock market before he retired and bought that Christmas tree ranch in New Mexico. But when it comes to people, he really can be *dumb*!"

"And you're smarter?" Pete laughed.

"I can spot a phony when I see one," said Allie. "The place my uncle bought once belonged to a mining company. There's a mine on it—Death Trap Mine."

"That's a great name," jeered Pete. "What was in the mine? Dinosaur bones?"

"Silver," said Allie. "The mine's dead now. The silver's all gone. It's called Death Trap Mine because a woman once wandered in there and fell down a shaft and was killed. Some of the old-timers in Twin Lakes—that's the town where

13

Uncle Harry's got his place—they say the woman's ghost still haunts the mine. Of course, I don't believe a word of that. But there *is* a spook around. He's the guy who bought the mine and a hunk of land around it from my uncle."

An angry spot of colour showed on Allie's tanned face. "He's up to something," she said. "He's playing some kind of game. He was born in Twin Lakes, see?"

"Is that a crime?" asked Bob, puzzled.

"No. But there's something funny about a guy who's born in a town and who leaves when he's practically a baby and then, years and years later, he comes back a millionaire and puts on this big act about how he's so glad to be home. Only he's about as friendly as a rattlesnake. Also, he opened the mine. The entrance was sealed with an iron grille, but he opened it and bought a guard dog to watch it. What is there to guard in a dead mine? The guy potters around the place in brand-new jeans and he's even got a hard hat, like construction workers wear. The get-up doesn't match the rest of him. He's got manicured nails!"

Allie paused. When the boys said nothing she went on with her recital. "He won't let anybody near that mine. I smell a rat. He's pulling some kind of fast one right in my uncle's front yard, and I'm going to figure out what it is."

"Lots of luck!" said Pete.

"Allie!" A man's voice came faintly to them. Bob went to the periscope that Jupe had rigged up and installed in the roof of the trailer so the boys could look out without being seen. He put his eye to it and peered across the piles of scrap. "There's a man with white hair and a big moustache near the gate. He's talking to Jupe's Aunt Mathilda," he reported.

"That's Uncle Harry." Allie slid off the desk. "I told him I'd be at the salvage yard. You guys want to meet him? He's nice—my favourite relative."

Allie marched to the sliding panel and out of the trailer. The boys suppressed triumphant grins as they followed her out. The panel was not the only secret entrance to Headquarters. At least the girl hadn't learned about the most important one— the trap-door in the office floor. The boys and Allie picked their way through the salvage to the front gate.

"There you are!" said Aunt Mathilda when she saw them. "I knew you were around somewhere. And Allie? How nice to see you again."

"I'm very glad to see you again, Mrs Jones," said Allie, in her most polite schoolgirl manner. "Uncle Harry, meet Jupiter Jones, Bob Andrews, and Pete Crenshaw."

"Hi," said Harrison Osborne. He shook Jupe's hand and nodded to Bob and Pete. "So you're The Three Investigators. Allie has told me about you."

"Nothing good, you can bet," said Allie.

The boys ignored Allie's remark. Jupe reached into his pocket and pulled out a large business card, which he handed to Harrison Osborne. "If you should ever have need of our services, sir . . ."

Mr Osborne read the card:

```
┌─────────────────────────────────────────┐
│                                           │
│     THE THREE INVESTIGATORS               │
│                                           │
│      "We Investigate Anything"            │
│                                           │
│         ?     ?     ?                     │
│                                           │
│     First Investigator – JUPITER JONES    │
│     Second Investigator – PETER CRENSHAW  │
│     Records and Research – BOB ANDREWS    │
│                                           │
└─────────────────────────────────────────┘
```

Allie's uncle handed the card back to Jupiter. "What do the question marks stand for?" he asked.

"The question mark is the universal symbol of the unknown," answered Jupe. "The three question marks on our card stand for The Three Investigators—they're our trademark. We specialize in solving any puzzles, riddles, mysteries, or enigmas brought to us."

"I doubt that I'll ever have a need for detectives in Twin Lakes," said Mr Osborne, with a chuckle. "But . . ." He was suddenly thoughtful. "But I *could* use three strong fellows like you at the ranch. And Allie really does need somebody nearer her own age . . . . Say, I don't suppose you boys have ever done any pruning?"

"Pruning?" echoed Bob. "Why sure."

"Good," said Uncle Harry. "Christmas trees have to be pruned or they won't be the right shape when they're harvested for Christmas. I've been having trouble getting help in Twin Lakes. Why don't you three come with Allie and me tomorrow morning and spend a couple of weeks at my ranch?

He turned to Aunt Mathilda. "If you could spare the boys for a while, I'd like to have them. We've got plenty of room, and I'll pay them by the hour, just as I'd pay anybody I got locally."

Aunt Mathilda looked doubtful. "I don't know." she said. "I thought that this week we might clear away that stack of salvage in the far corner of the yard. It's only taking up room."

All three boys started. Aunt Mathilda was planning to remove the heaps of junk that protected Headquarters! Jupe thought quickly. Without the boys, she would never get to this task.

"Aunt Mathilda. I would like very much to go with Allie and her uncle. It would be a new experience."

"And new experiences are good for you!" said Allie, laughing. "Besides, you just might run into some mystery in Twin Lakes, and that would be fun!"

Jupe suddenly realized that in some devious way Allie had put her uncle up to issuing the invitation. She had trapped them into helping her with her case.

"It might be fun at that," said Pete. "I think my folks will let me go."

Bob looked eager. "I *know* I can get leave of absence from my part-time job at the library. It's slow there now."

"Well, all right," said Aunt Mathilda.

Harrison Osborne shook her hand. "I promise not to work the boys too hard."

"I'm not worried about that," said Aunt Mathilda. "It can't be done. They can think of more excuses not to work than a centipede has legs!"

2

A Roaring Welcome

"Such as it is, this is Twin Lakes," announced Harrison Osborne.

He slowed the big air-conditioned station wagon that had carried them across the Arizona deserts and up into the hills of south-western New Mexico. The boys, who rode in the back, looked ahead along the tar-macadamed logging road and saw a green valley between two ranges of tree-covered mountains. There were rows of little frame houses on dusty streets that ran back from the main road. Several buildings faced the road—a grocer's store, a drugstore, a newspaper office, and a tiny crumbling hardware store. In the centre of town a faded brick courthouse reared up to an imposing two storeys. There was a filling station and, beyond this, the Twin Lakes Fire Department.

"Fire!" said Pete suddenly, pointing to a place beyond town. Smoke curled up into the clear afternoon air.

"Don't panic," said Allie. She sat next to her uncle in the front seat. "That's just smoke from the furnace at the sawmill."

"Mining used to be the big thing here," Uncle Harry told them. "Now the mines are all played out and the sawmill keeps the town going. Logging is the only thing left. Forty-five years ago Twin Lakes was a rip-roaring place, but no more."

"Last place in the world I'd come to if I wanted to pull a fast one," said Pete.

Harrison Osborne looked away from the road for a second. "A fast one?" he said. "Allie, have you been telling the boys any of your wild tales?"

Allie stared straight ahead.

"*Allie?*" Her uncle stopped the car to let a woman dressed in jeans and a plaid shirt cross the road in front of him.

"I only said that Wesley Thurgood is a phony—and he is, Uncle Harry!"

Uncle Harry made a sound that was halfway between a snort and a laugh. He kept his foot on the brake and turned to face the boys. "I know you three are amateur detectives," he said, "but don't go bothering Wesley Thurgood. He is our neighbour and I don't want any trouble with neighbours. Thurgood's got a fine reputation. He's made a lot of money in real estate, and he came back to Twin Lakes because that's where he started out. He was born here—just before the mine closed down. His family moved away soon after, but he told me he grew up hearing exciting stories of Twin Lakes' boom-town days. He bought Death Trap Mine because his father once worked there. Now that doesn't seem to me like such a far-out thing to do."

"So why'd he open up the mine again?" demanded Allie with all the authority she could muster.

"That's none of our business," said her uncle.

"I do know that it wasn't so kids could prowl around and maybe get hurt. Thurgood's one hundred per-cent aboveboard. I've checked him out and so has my bank. He's a millionaire—his credit rating would make a Vanderbilt look poverty-stricken."

He turned to the boys and smiled. "Allie has a way of going off half-cocked," he said. "She's got it in for Thurgood because she tried to explore the mine one day and he marched her back home by the scruff of the neck. And quite rightly. It's called Death Trap Mine because a woman was killed in there years ago on just that sort of an expedition."

Pete exploded with laughter. "Allie! You didn't tell us you got thrown off Thurgood's place!"

"Oh, shut up!" Allie's voice shook with anger.

Jupe chuckled as he pictured the proud girl being marched out of the mine.

"He's a phony, I tell you!" cried Allie.

"Perhaps he's only eccentric," said Jupe. "Wealthy people sometimes *are* eccentric."

"That's no crime," said Uncle Harry. He released the brake and they were moving again. "I don't want you to bother him again, Allie. And that goes for you, too, boys."

The car turned off the tar-macadamed road and bumped across a wooden bridge that spanned a tiny waterfall between two lakes that were hardly more than ponds. The boys guessed that these gave the town its name. Beyond the road was a dirt track and dust billowed out behind the car. About a mile from the bridge, on the left side of

21

the road, were fields filled with young evergreens and, farther on, an open gate. Across the road from the gate sat several small houses. One was newly painted, but the others looked desolate and abandoned. Uncle Harry slowed and honked the horn at a tall, lean woman who was watering the garden next to the trim little house.

"That's Mrs Macomber," said Allie.

The woman smiled and waved at them. She wore dark slacks, a white shirt, and a massive Indian necklace of silver and turquoise. When she moved back to turn off her hose, the boys could see that although her black hair was streaked with silver and she must have been at least sixty, she moved as easily as a young girl.

"She was born here way back in the boom days," said Allie. "She married the superintendent of the mine. They moved away after the mine closed down. When her husband died she worked in Phoenix to save enough money to come back and buy the house she had lived in as a bride. She owns those other places, too—the little run-down houses —but she doesn't use them for anything."

"So her story's not so different from Wesley Thurgood's, is it?" said Bob.

"That's not the point," snapped Allie. "Mrs Macomber is a nice lady."

"That *is* the point," said Uncle Harry. "Twin Lakes is a great place to live and a perfect place to retire." He stopped the car outside the open gate and pointed ahead to where the road ended and steep mountains edged the western side of the valley. In a hillside towards the left, about a quarter of a mile away, the boys could see an opening—a black timber-framed square.

"That's Death Trap Mine," said Uncle Harry. "The cabin up there is where Mr Thurgood lives. And he also owns that big building behind it. It used to be the mine works."

The boys nodded as Uncle Harry turned left through the gate on to a narrow, rutted drive. Rows of small Christmas trees spread out on both sides. The car bounced past a fenced pasture on the right, where Allie's horse, a handsome Appaloosa named Indian Queen, grazed together with three other horses. Farther down the drive, on the left, a spanking new ranch-house sat in a clearing among the low trees. It was cedar red with immaculate white trim. At the end of the drive was an ancient sagging barn that had not been painted for many years.

Uncle Harry stopped the car in front of the ranch-house, yawned, and stretched. "Home at last," he said.

The boys and Allie tumbled out of the station wagon, and the boys stood for a moment and looked around. A dusty, no-nonsense pick-up truck was parked in front of the barn. On the far side of the house they could see the edge of a fenced enclosure where chickens clucked and scratched.

Uncle Harry got out from behind the steering wheel, moving rather stiffly. "I like my eggs real fresh," he said, pointing towards the hen-yard. "Besides, there's something kind of peaceful about waking up in the morning and hearing them cluck around. And I *do* wake up in the morning because the rooster thinks it's his personal responsibility to start the day."

The words were scarcely spoken before the rooster could be heard from behind the house. He wasn't crowing—he was squawking.

A split second later there was a screeching, fluttering, flapping uproar in the hen-yard. An instant after that the boys heard the thunderous explosion of a gun.

Pete shouted and fell to the ground, instinctively covering his head with his arms. Jupe and Bob ducked behind the car.

A huge dark shape came racing from behind the hen-yard and bounded towards Jupe. Jupe had a confused impression of gleaming white teeth and dark eyes. Then the creature leaped, knocked him to the ground, and bounded over him to disappear westwards into a field of Christmas trees.

3

Allie's Mysterious Millionaire

"WELCOME TO PEACEFUL ACRES!" laughed Allie, as the afternoon stillness settled over the ranch again.

Pete sat up and blinked. "What the heck was that?" he demanded.

"Just Wesley Thurgood's monster of a guard dog having another go at the chickens," Allie explained as Jupiter picked himself up. "He tries to dig his way under the fence into the chicken-yard. The chickens squawk and Magdalena runs out and shoots off her shotgun. If that dog doesn't watch it, she just might stop shooting into the air, and he'll have a tail full of buckshot."

"Magdalena?" said Bob.

"My housekeeper," explained Uncle Harry.

A stout black-haired Mexican woman came round from behind the house. She wore a dress made of course cotton fabric with bright flowers embroidered at the neck and on the sleeves, and she carried a shotgun.

"Senor Osborne!" she cried. "Allie! I am pleased you are back. It is too quiet when you are not here."

Harrison Osborne chuckled. "So you have your

25

own ways of livening things up," he said.

Magdalena scowled. "That dog, he is a thief!"

"Never mind," said Uncle Harry. "Keep blasting away with that gun and he'll reform. Magdalena, these boys are friends of Allie's. Jupiter Jones, Bob Andrews, and Pete Crenshaw. They're going to stay with us for a couple of weeks."

Magdalena's black eyes sparkled. "Ah, good, good!" she cried. "It is nice to have more young people here. I will get steaks from the freezer. You are hungry after your journey."

She disappeared into the house.

"I hope you *are* hungry after your journey," said Uncle Harry. "Magdalena doesn't have any patience with people who pick at their food."

"Don't worry!" said Jupe heartily.

Uncle Harry began to take suitcases out of the station wagon and set them on the front porch. The boys hurried to help him. In a few minutes they had carried their things into the house and upstairs to a big bunkroom directly above the spacious living room. Allie's room was on the first floor, next to her uncle's. Magdalena had her own little apartment behind the kitchen.

"You'll want to wash up," Uncle Harry called to them as they began to unpack. "Don't take too long. I'd like to show you around the place before dinner."

Pete immediately lost interest in stowing his clothes in the closet. "We can unpack anytime," he said, heading for the bath across the landing from the bunkroom.

Soon the boys, Allie, and Uncle Harry were out

26

under the blue New Mexico sky. Allie ran down the drive, two lumps of sugar in her hand. "Here, Queenie," she called. Her Appaloosa snorted and galloped to the fence. The girl hugged the horse's neck and it tossed its head, whinnying joyfully.

"Getting Allie off that horse's back, even for a couple of days, was quite a job," said Harrison Osborne, "C'mon. I want to show you the machetes we use for pruning."

"Machetes?" said Pete. "Aren't they big knives?"

Uncle Harry nodded. "In adventure stories, the heroes use them to hack a path through the jungle." He led the boys past the pick-up truck and opened the door of the dilapidated barn. The boys smelled hay and saw bales piled high in one corner. Coils of hose hung from pegs in the wall. Spades, shears, trowels, and hoes were neatly stacked beside a workbench which had a grindstone fastened to it. Over the workbench was a rack with five, huge, deadly-looking knives.

"We always use shears when we prune at home," said Pete.

"With thousands of Christmas trees to be done, shears are too slow," Uncle Harry told him. "Besides, you can really get a good sweep with a machete." He took down one of the great knives, stepped away from the boys, and demonstrated. "The trees don't grow to be a perfect Christmas-tree shape naturally," he said. "When I bought this place three years ago. I thought all I'd have to do was stick little trees into the ground and wait for them to get big. There's more to it. You've got to irrigate and kill weeds, and you have to prune. You look at a tree and picture it the way a Christmas tree should look—nice and tapering, full at the bottom and small at the top. Then you take aim and bring the machete down like this—" The blade flashed and the air swooshed as Uncle Harry's arm came down in a slanting motion. "You cut off anything that's going to interfere with that nice shape. But be careful, because if you make a mistake with a machete you can open a king-sized gash in your leg. I prune in the summer and by the time my trees are ready to be harvested in November, the new growth has come out to cover the cuts and the trees are fuller. Got it?"

"Right," said Pete.

Uncle Harry carefully put the machete back in its place and pointed to a dusty old automobile that stood on solid rubber tyres in the far side of the barn. "One of these days I'm going to build a new barn," he said, "and that car is another thing I'm going to do something about."

Jupe went to the car and peered through a half-opened window. He saw seats covered with cracked black leather, and bare wooden floorboards. "It's a Model T Ford, isn't it?" he asked.

"It is," said Uncle Harry. "I got it as kind of a bonus when I bought this place. It was standing right there, half-covered with hay. I got as far as getting the hay off, and then I had to forget it. I've been too busy. But when I can, I'm going to restore it. Model T's are collectors' items today."

Allie appeared at the open door. "Wesley Thurgood's coming down the drive," she announced.

"Okay, Allie. You behave yourself," warned Uncle Harry. "No smart talk, you hear?"

Allie didn't answer. The boys heard footsteps outside and a voice called. "Mr Osborne?"

"In here," said Uncle Harry.

A thin fortyish man with blond wavy hair came into the barn. He wore jeans that were so new they were stiff, and boots that were gleaming and un-scuffed. His western shirt looked as if it had been taken out of the box that afternoon. Jupe watched him shake hands with Uncle Harry, then listened as he apologized for the intrusion of his watchdog. Jupe felt that in at least one of her accusations Allie had been right. Thurgood *did* look like a person who was playing a part—an actor who had costumed himself for a role. But then Jupe reflec-ted. What else would anyone wear in a place like Twin Lakes but jeans and boots and a western shirt? And if Wesley Thurgood didn't have old jeans, what would be more natural than to buy new ones?

"I've chained the dog up," said Thurgood. "He won't be down here to bother you again."

"It's no big deal," said Uncle Harry. "So long as he doesn't actually get any of the chickens, and I don't think he will with Magdalena around."

Uncle Harry then introduced the boys. Allie ig-nored Thurgood and stared into space. He glanced at her briefly, and his clear blue eyes became hard for a second. Then he seemed to look right through her to the Model T. "Say, that's quite a rare car you've got there," he said.

"I was just telling the boys I'm going to fix it

up one of these days," said Uncle Harry.

Wesley Thurgood stepped over to touch the car, and suddenly Pete straightened.

"Wesley Thurgood!" he exclaimed. "I thought I'd heard that name before!"

"Eh?" said Thurgood.

"My father does special effects for the movies," said Pete. "He was talking about you at dinner a while back, Mr Thurgood. He said the props department at his studio needed an old Reo for a picture they were making, and they got it from you. You're an old car buff."

"Oh? Oh, yes, that's right," said Thurgood.

"Dad was telling us about your collection of old cars," said Pete. "He said you've got a private garage where you keep them and a full-time mechanic who doesn't do anything except make sure they're in running condition."

"Yes," said Thurgood. "Well, why not? They don't make them like they used to, do they?"

"Wasn't it your Silver Cloud that was used in the movie *The Fortune Hunters?*" Pete asked.

"Silver Cloud? Why, yes. I did let one of the studios borrow that not . . . not long ago."

"A Silver Cloud?" said Uncle Harry. "Guess my Model T looks pretty humble."

"I started small, too," said Thurgood. "Once you really get the old car bug, you'll probably start buying. You'll have to enlarge your barn."

"You mean I'll have to build a new one," said Uncle Harry, and he and Thurgood strolled out of the place with Uncle Harry talking excitedly of his plans for his ranch.

"Well?" said Allie, when the two men were gone. "Have you ever seen such a phony?"

"So his clothes are new," said Pete. "So what? I didn't remember the name Wesley Thurgood until he got so interested in the Model T, but my dad talked a lot about him and his car collection. He's got piles of dough and he's kind of a recluse—has a big house in Mandeville Canyon with ten-foot walls around it."

Jupiter cleared his throat. "He did not, however, lend a Silver Cloud to be used in the filming of *The Fortune Hunters*," said Jupe, in the somewhat stuffy manner he used when imparting information. "There was an article in *Film Fun* about that car. It didn't belong to Thurgood. It belonged to Jonathan Carrington, the financier. Also, *The Fortune Hunters* was not filmed recently. That picture has been out for several years."

No one contradicted Jupe, who prided himself on his knowledge of motion pictures and the theatre. But Allie Jamison crowed in triumph. "What did I tell you? A phony! He lied!"

Jupe smiled. "Not necessarily, Allie. You're jumping to conclusions again. Wesley Thurgood is a very wealthy man, and if he owns a fleet of antique automobiles and has a man whose exclusive duty is to take care of them, he would hardly be bothered with details. He might not remember whether he loaned a certain car to a studio at a certain time. No doubt some employee takes care of the negotiations and the mechanic delivers the car to the studio."

"Ha!" said Allie, since there seemed to be

nothing more clever to say in reply.

There was a rather stiff silence in the barn until Magdalena could be heard calling the four young people for dinner.

4

Shots in the Dark

"HAVE MORE STRAWBERRY SHORTCAKE," said Magdalena from her end of the long table in the big kitchen. Jupe had just finished the last crumb of his dessert.

"No thanks," he said. "It was delicious, but I'm trying to take off some weight."

Magdalena frowned, "You young people—always you worry about weight. Allie, she eats like a sparrow, so she is skinny like a little stick. This summer I try to make her plump like a pigeon."

"You've got it all wrong, Magdalena," said Allie. "The American Medical Association says skinny is the thing to be. Baby Fatso here," and she nodded towards Jupe, "should pay attention."

Jupe reddened. He hated to be reminded of the time when he had been a child star, distinctly on the plump side, and known from coast to coast as Baby Fatso.

"I diet all the time," said Jupe.

"You mean when you're not actually eating." Allie stood up and carried her dishes to the sink.

"Allie, you are a rotten hostess and if you were a little younger than you are I'd turn you over my

33

knee and paddle you," her uncle told her.

Allie didn't answer. She rinsed her dishes and put them into the dishwater.

Magdalena got up from the table. "Go and talk with your friends. I will do those."

"We can help, Magdalena," Bob offered.

"No, no! I do not like a crowd in my kitchen. Besides, there is the dishwasher and it does the work."

Uncle Harry, Allie, and the boys retreated to the living room, where Uncle Harry promptly fell asleep in front of the television set. Soon the boys were yawning.

"Deadheads!" jeered Allie. "It's not even nine o'clock."

"We were up at five this morning," Bob reminded her.

"So was I," said Allie. "Tell you what. I'll get out the chessboard and . . ."

"No thanks!" Jupe interrupted. "I have decided that according to my own official clock, which is inside my head, it is ten-thirty. I am going to bed."

"Me, too." Pete started for the stairs.

Bob yawned and went after him.

"Spoilsports!" Allie taunted.

"That Allie can be a pain in the neck," Pete complained, when the boys were upstairs and getting into bed. "She never runs out of steam."

Jupe stretched out and put his hands behind his head. "I'm not so sure," he said. "Listen."

Bob and Pete were silent. They heard the muted sound of the television being turned off. Harrison

Osborne's voice came to them, low and sleepy. A door closed and water ran in a shower. Then another door closed.

"Allie's going to bed, too," said Jupe.

He turned over on his side and turned off the bedside lamp. The room was dark, except for the moonlight which came through the open windows and threw cold squares of light on the floor.

Jupiter closed his eyes. In a second he was asleep. He slept deeply, not stirring, until he was jarred awake by a noise that came from outside—a muffled roar that echoed and rumbled and then died away.

Instantly alert, Jupe sat up. He concentrated, listening for a repetition of the sound.

In his bunk, Pete groaned. "Magdalena," he mumbled. "Shooting at the dog again."

"No." Jupe got out of bed and went to the window. "It sounded like a shot, but it wasn't Magdalena. Too far away."

Jupiter looked out over the moonlit fields of Christmas trees stretching away from the house. To his right, he could see Mrs Macomber's house and the abandoned dwellings that made up her little domain. Straight ahead, Wesley Thurgood's property was fully visible on the rising slope of land. A small, square-shaped truck was parked near the mine entrance. A shadow moved next to Thurgood's cabin, and the guard dog prowled to the end of his chain, lifted his head, and howled.

A light went on in the little house across from Uncle Harry's gate. A door opened and Jupe saw Mrs Macomber come out in a dressing gown. She stood on the porch and looked up towards Thurgood's place.

There were voices in the living room below. Uncle Harry was up, and so was Magdalena.

"It was not me," the boys heard the housekeeper say. "I did not shoot the gun."

Bare feet thudded on the stairway, and there was a pounding at the door. "Hey, you guys!" It was Allie. "Did you hear that?"

The Three Investigators got into their dressing gowns and went out on the landing. Allie was kneeling at the window there with her elbows on the sill. "It's Thurgood!" whispered Allie. "I'm sure that shot came from Thurgood's place. And look!"

Pete went to the window. "What is it?" he asked.

Allie pointed across to Mrs Macomber's house. The woman on the porch turned, went inside, and shut the door.

"The sound woke Mrs Macomber," Allie pointed out. "And it woke the dog. He barked. And it woke us. But it didn't wake Thurgood. At least he didn't put on any lights and he didn't go out to calm the dog down. I'll bet it was him shooting!"

"Allie!" Harrison Osborne's voice came from below. "What are you doing up there?"

"Just seeing what I can see," called Allie. She got up and went to the top of the staircase. "Uncle Harry, I'm sure that was Wesley Thurgood shooting,"

"Allie," said her uncle wearily, "you're getting to be a nut about Thurgood. It was probably somebody out hunting jack rabbits or coyotes."

"Who?" demanded Allie. "From here I can see all the way to the hills. There isn't anybody out. Besides, if there's a coyote around, wouldn't he be trying to get at our chickens?"

"Not if somebody shot at him first," said Uncle Harry. "Now you come down here and go back to bed, and let the boys get their sleep."

"Oh, blast!" exclaimed Allie.

She had started down the stairs when Jupe suddenly called her back to the window.

Thurgood had appeared in the clearing near his cabin. A shotgun was cradled in his arms. The boys saw him gaze at the hills across the road from his property. Then he put the gun to his shoulder, took aim, and fired.

Again the sound of a shot broke the night stillness. Again the dog howled. Thurgood went to him and patted him on the head. The dog stopped barking, and Thurgood disappeared into his cabin.

"You were right about one thing, Allie," said Pete. "It was Thurgood."

"And it looks like your uncle was right about another," Bob pointed out. "He must have been firing at a coyote."

Allie made an indignant noise and flounced down the stairs.

"Allie sure has it in for Thurgood," said Bob, as he padded back into the bunkroom. "No matter what he does, she decides he's up to no good."

Jupiter got into bed. "I think that if I owned a mine, I would escort Allie Jamison on an inspection tour so that she could satisfy her curiosity,"

37

he said. "It would be so much easier than making an enemy of her."

Bob and Pete climbed into bed, and in a few minutes their steady breathing told Jupe that they were asleep. But Jupiter found himself oddly wakeful. The First Investigator lay in the darkness and listened to the wind rustle the Christmas trees.

Finally Jupe sat up. "Where was Thurgood when he fired that first shot?" he said aloud.

"Hm?" Pete turned over in bed.

"Wha . . . what?" said Bob.

"Where was Thurgood when he fired the first shot?"

"The first shot?" said Pete "In his house, I suppose."

"Did you see him come out?" Jupe asked. "Did you see him come into the yard before that second shot?"

"No. I guess not. I was watching Allie."

"So was I," said Jupe. "Bob, did you see where Thurgood came from before he fired again?"

"No, I didn't," said Bob.

"So he could have been anyplace," Jupe concluded. "I don't think he was in his house. The first shot was muffled, so much so that I wasn't even sure it *was* a shot. The second one was clearer and it sounded nearer. I think Thurgood was in the mine when he fired that first shot."

"So what?" asked Pete.

"Nothing, perhaps," said Jupe, "except that I don't think there was a coyote. The dog would have barked at a coyote, and we would have heard him. But the dog didn't bark until after the shot. What if Thurgood shot at something in the mine and then came out and found that the noise had roused the neighbours. Suppose he didn't want anyone to know he was shooting in the mine. What would he do?"

The other two boys didn't answer.

"Wouldn't he stand out in the open and shoot again?" asked Jupe. "Wouldn't he want it to appear that he *was* shooting at a coyote?"

"You're getting as bad as Allie," said Bob.

"That may be," Jupe admitted. "But it is also possible that there is something a bit odd about Mr Thurgood. Perhaps Allie *does* have a case after all!"

5

The Forbidden Mine

WHEN JUPE WOKE to see sunshine, his suspicions of the night before seemed ridiculous. He dressed and went down to the kitchen, where Bob and Pete were already eating. Uncle Harry sat at the head of the table, and Magdalena was at the stove pouring pancake batter on to a griddle.

Pete lifted a hand in greeting. "Allie's out riding and we were about to come up and wake you," he said, "Today we get to do our stuff with the machetes."

"That will be a change," said Jupe.

"A change from what?" asked Uncle Harry.

"From moving junk around The Jones Salvage Yard!" Jupe told him.

"I hope you enjoy it." Uncle Harry smiled. "I do. It's kind of creative to think that you're carving a Christmas tree. Don't work like slaves the first day though. Just go at it for an hour or so at a time, then rest."

After breakfast Uncle Harry took down three of the great knives that hung over the workbench in the barn. The boys followed him to a field between the ranch-house and the road. They watched as he pruned a tree, bringing the machete

40

down in quick slanting strokes to cut away branches that grew out in odd places. "Don't get too close to the tree," he warned. "Stand back away from the machete, and always swing the knife off and to one side. I don't want any accidents."

Uncle Harry watched while each of the boys pruned a tree. When he was satisfied that they had the hang of it, he left them in the field and went back to the house. A few minutes later he drove off in the station wagon with Magdalena.

The boys worked in silence until they heard the hoofbeats of Allie's Appaloosa pounding in the fields between the drive and Wesley Thurgood's property. As the boys looked up, Allie rode on into the pasture, unsaddled the mare, and rubbed it down with handfuls of straw. Then she disappeared into the ranch-house.

Before long the boys heard the sound of a car starting. They looked towards the barn. "Oh, wow!" Pete said, "What next?" Allie had climbed behind the steering wheel of her uncle's pick-up truck. Gears clashed and Allie and the truck came lurching down the drive.

"Allie, you nut!" yelled Pete. "What are you doing?"

Allie came abreast of the boys and stepped on the brake. The engine coughed and died. "It's okay," said Allie cheerfully. "I can drive it, so long as I don't take it off the ranch."

"You're too young!" protested Bob.

"I'm too young to get a licence," said Allie. "But as long as I can reach the pedals, I'm not too

41

young to drive Uncle Harry's pick-up truck."

She tried to start the truck again and failed. "Need more practice, I guess," said Allie.

"Does your uncle know you do that?" asked Pete.

"Sure!" Allie answered. "He thinks girls should know how to do everything guys can do."

"I'll bet," said Pete. "That's why you waited until he and Magdalena left."

Allie leaned out of the cab. Her eyes were dancing. "They've gone to the store and they won't be back for a while. And Wesley Thurgood isn't home either, and the dog is chained up."

"I know what you're thinking," said Pete. "You want to explore that mine. Well, you're on your own."

Jupe stood holding a machete. He remembered the sound of the shot in the night—a muffled sound that might have come from a tunnel in the mountainside.

"Stick-in-the-muds!" jeered Allie. "Okay! Stay there and forget about the mystery." The truck engine ground again, and this time it caught.

"Wait a second!" shouted Jupe. "I'll go with you!"

"Good!" Allie laughed. "Bring your machete along. If Thurgood comes back, we'll run back to the truck and pretend to be pruning in the field near his place. What about you, Pete? And Bob?"

Pete looked doubtfully at Jupiter. The tallest and most athletic of the Investigators, Pete enjoyed physical adventures—but he hated walking into trouble. Jupe, on the other hand, could not resist investigating any mystery, no matter how slight, no matter what the danger. And once he had decided to act, he couldn't be stopped. Shrugging, Pete climbed into the cab next to Allie. Bob, too, realized that Jupiter was on the trail of something, and followed him into the back of the truck.

Allie got the pick-up started again, and they went bouncing off through the fields on a rough dirt track that had been bulldozed across Harrison Osborne's property.

"This is a great truck," Allie exclaimed. She was so busy trying to control it that she seemed to be in action from the top of her head to the soles of her feet. She had to slouch low every time she put the clutch in, and push mightily on the gearshift lever. Her hand flashed out to touch a second lever next to the gear shift. "That's to convert it to four-wheel drive, in case you go up into the hills and need the extra power," she said. "And there's a winch on the front in case you get stuck or go into a ditch. And it's got four, forward speeds. The diagram for the gear shift is on the lever. You push it up there for first and then pull it towards you for second and . . ."

". . . And I only hope we get it back to the barn in one piece!" said Pete as the truck lurched forwards.

"You worry too much," said Allie. She stopped the truck at the edge of the field that bordered Wesley Thurgood's property. The boys climbed out of the vehicle and stood looking around.

43

Across a bare stretch of ground they saw the mountainside jut up abruptly. The mine entrance was a dark, threatening hole at the base of it. They could see a few feet into the mine, past the timbers that framed the entrance. There was dry white sand and some gravel on the floor of the mine tunnel. The tunnel itself seemed to slope downwards away from the entrance. To the right of the mine was the decaying cabin where Thurgood lived.

"Crummy, huh?" Allie said, pointing.

"He'll probably fix it up sooner or later," said Bob. "How long has he been here?"

"Almost a month," Allie told him. "He moved in with a bedroll and some pots and pans, and I think that's all he's got now. He's really roughing it. That big building behind his cabin used to be the mine works. That's where they took the ore from the mine and separated out the silver."

A chain rattled and the guard dog came around the corner of the cabin. He was not as enormous as the boys had thought at first, but he was a very large dog. Jupe guessed that he was part Labrador retriever and part German shepherd. When he saw Allie and the boys, he gave a low growl.

"You sure that chain he's got on is attached to something real solid?" said Pete.

Allie laughed. "Don't worry. I threw a stick at him before, when I rode past on Queenie. He can't get at us."

"I like the way you make friends with dumb animals, Allie," said Bob. "Suppose he'd gotten loose?"

44

"Then Queenie and I would have outrun him," declared Allie. She took a flashlight from the glove compartment of the pick-up. "Come on."

They started across the clearing to the mine entrance. The dog went into a frenzy, flinging himself at them, trying with all his might to break his chain. Allie ignored him, and The Three Investigators followed her into the brooding gloom of the mine.

When they were a few feet past the entrance, Allie snapped on the light. Its beam darted along the floor of the tunnel, which slanted downwards. Side passages went off at intervals. The walls were braced with timbers as big as railway sleepers, and huge crossbeams helped support the rocky ceiling.

Apart from the sound of the dog barking outside, the mine was perfectly quiet. Yet somehow there was a faint air of menace all round. Allie and the boys moved slowly along the tunnel, picking their way on the rocky, uneven floor. Jupe kept his eyes fixed on the beam of light as it probed the waiting darkness ahead.

About fifty yards into the mountain, the tunnel branched out and became two tunnels, one leading off to the right and one extending at a slight angle to the left. They hesitated. Then Allie started towards the left. The boys followed and the feeble light from the mine entrance was gone. Except for the flashlight, they were in total darkness. Their footsteps echoed eerily in the tunnel.

"I wonder where the lady fell," said Allie. "The one who was killed in here."

In spite of herself, she shivered.

"Wait a minute, Allie," said Jupe. He had glimpsed something on the floor of the tunnel. "Shine the light over here a second, would you?" he asked.

Allie flashed the beam of light on a little heap of loose rock and pebbles. They seemed to have fallen from the wall of the tunnel. As Jupe bent to pick up a small stone, Allie and the light abruptly moved away.

"Hey!" shouted Pete. "Come back with that flash!"

Allie kept going, the flashlight bobbing and glowing ever more faintly from a side corridor that she had dodged into.

"Allie!" called Bob.

Suddenly there was a light in the tunnel behind them—a very powerful light that caught the boys and held them in its glare. "Exactly what do you kids think you're doing?" demanded an angry voice—the voice of Wesley Thurgood.

"Uh-oh!" said Pete.

Then The Three Investigators heard Allie drop her flashlight. It clattered against some rocks and they heard glass breaking.

At the end of that darkened corridor, Allie let out a blood-curdling scream.

She screamed and screamed and screamed.

6

Death Trap!

"ALLIE! WHAT IS IT?" shouted Jupe.

The screams went on, high and hysterical.

"Blast that brat!" Thurgood dashed past the boys and plunged into the side corridor. The boys stumbled after him.

Allie was there, standing stiffly at the edge of a pit that gaped in the floor of the mine. She stared down into the darkness at her feet and she screamed.

"Stop that!" Thurgood seized her arm and pulled her back away from the pit.

Allie trembled and pointed towards the pit. "D-d-d-down there!"

The boys went cautiously to the edge of the shaft and Thurgood shone his light down. The pit was not deep—only ten or twelve feet—but the walls were sheer, straight up and down.

At the bottom of the hole was something that looked like a heap of old clothes. But then, in the light of the torch, they could all see what had once been a hand—a human hand. There was a body inside the clothes, a body that lay strangely twisted on the rocky floor of the shaft. They saw hollow eyes and a dusty, matted tangle of hair.

"Dead!" cried Allie. "He's . . . it's dead! Dead!"

"Stop that!" snapped Thurgood again.

Allie gulped and was quiet.

"Now get out!" ordered Thurgood. "All of you!"

Jupiter and Bob grabbed Allie's arms. With Pete stumbling behind them and Thurgood herding them along with his flashlight, they made their way back to the main mine tunnel and then out through the entrance into the sunlight. The dog barked, but it seemed to Jupe that the sound was unreal—part of a nightmare. In his mind Jupe kept seeing the crumple of clothing at the bottom of the shaft, the head with the staring eyes, and the skinny, leathery hand.

"You kids get home!" said Thurgood. "Get home and stay there, all of you. If I ever catch you in my mine again, I'll . . . I'll . . ."

He walked quickly to his cabin and slammed the door closed. Allie and the boys moved off slowly, past Thurgood's shiny red Chevy Suburban "truck," which was now parked near the mine, past Uncle Harry's pick-up, which they left standing in the field.

By the time they reached the ranch-house, colour had come back to Allie's face. "We'll call the sheriff," she said. "That Thurgood! I knew there was something spooky about him!"

"I am sure he has already called the sheriff," Jupe told her. "I am also sure that you'd better not accuse him of anything."

"Why not?" said Allie. "There's a dead man in his mine!"

48

"And at the moment we have no idea how that dead man got there," Jupe pointed out.

A cloud of dust soon appeared on the road to town. A second later a tan sedan sped past. The word "Sheriff" was stencilled on the door panel. The boys glimpsed the driver, a big man wearing a stetson. The car turned in towards Thurgood's cabin and halted.

Jupe smiled. "You see?" he said to Allie.

Allie smiled back, but her smile was malicious. "I wonder what Thurgood's going to tell the sheriff."

"What are you going to tell your uncle?" Jupe nodded towards the road. The station wagon was approaching, with Uncle Harry and Magdalena in the front seat. Uncle Harry turned in at the gate, and Jupe could see that he looked concerned.

"Allie!" he called. The car came to a stop in the drive and Uncle Harry leaned out the window. "Sheriff Tait passed me on the road. Is anything wrong?"

"There's a body in Thurgood's mine," said Allie smugly.

"A body? In the mine?"

Allie nodded.

"*Madre de Dios!*" Magdalena got out of the station wagon. "Allie, how do you know this?"

There was an uncomfortable silence. Harrison Osborne looked at his niece. "Allie, were you in that mine again?"

Jupe took a step forward and answered Uncle Harry's question. "Yes, we all were, Mr Osborne. I was curious about those shots last night, and . . ."

"I don't want to hear any explanations!" said Uncle Harry. "I want you all to go into the house and stay there, do you understand?"

Uncle Harry stamped away across the fields, heading for Thurgood's property. As he went he was joined by Mrs Macomber, who had come out of her house when the sheriff's car passed.

The Three Investigators and Allie prowled from window to window on the second floor of the ranch-house, trying to catch a glimpse of any action. After a time an ambulance drove up to Thurgood's property and backed up to the mine entrance. It was more than an hour before it left and disappeared towards town. In the meantime several other cars arrived. One of them belonged to the highway patrol. At three, Harrison Osborne returned to the ranch-house in his pick-up truck.

"Well?" said Allie. "Did they arrest Thurgood?"

"Certainly not," said Uncle Harry. "Why should they arrest him? Whoever that was in the mine, he's been dead for a long, long time. The coroner's going to do an autopsy, but it looks as if the dead man got in there years ago, fell down that shaft, and broke his neck. It's got nothing to do with Thurgood. It must have happened before the mine entrance was sealed."

"Five years ago," said Magdalena, who had come in from the kitchen. "The poor soul. For five years he has been there, and no one to know it!"

"Is that when the mine was sealed?" asked Pete. "I thought it closed down forty years ago."

"You are right, Pete," said Magdalena. "The mine closed down long ago, but people could still get inside. *Si*. It was five years ago—in the springtime—they shut it with an iron grille. I remember it."

Jupe sat on the floor, absent-mindedly tossing a pebble into the air.

"What is that?" Allie asked him.

Jupe caught the pebble. "I picked it up in the mine this morning, before you went off with the flashlight." He wet one finger on his tongue and rubbed the pebble. "You told me Death Trap is a played-out silver mine," he said. "Was there gold in it, too?"

"Not that I ever heard of," said Uncle Harry.

Jupe held the pebble towards the light. "It has a small bright streak," he said. "Probably just iron pyrite. They call it fool's gold."

"I don't care about iron pyrite," said Allie. "What I want to know is why Wesley Thurgood didn't report that body in the mine. We had to go in and find it before he was forced to call the sheriff. I mean, once we'd seen the corpse, what else could he do?"

Uncle Harry was losing his patience. "Wesley Thurgood did not *know* the body was in the mine," he said. "He removed the iron grille from the entrance only last week, and he hasn't had time to explore the mine thoroughly. Allie, he had no reason to conceal that body. If you don't stop making wild accusations you'll force me to lock you in the cellar and tie a sack over your head!"

A car pulled up in the drive outside, and the

sheriff came across the porch. Magdalena had the door open for him before he could knock. Uncle Harry stood up, but the sheriff looked at Allie. His gaze was stern. "Allie, you know why they call that mine a death trap?"

Allie nodded.

"People can get killed there, can't they?"

Again Allie nodded. "I know, Sheriff Tait."

"If you ever go in there again, I'll arrest you and take you down to the courthouse and your uncle will have to come and get you. That goes for you, too, boys."

Sheriff Tait took a chair across from Uncle Harry.

"Did you find out who that man was?" Harrison Osborne asked.

Tait nodded. "I think so. There was a wallet in the hip pocket with an identification card that had a San Francisco address. We telephoned San Francisco to see if the police there had a missing-persons report on a Gilbert Morgan who might have disappeared five years ago, or perhaps even longer ago than that. They sure did. In January, more than five years ago. Gilbert Morgan, who has also used the names George Milling, Glenn Mercer, and George Martins, was released from San Quentin after serving six years of a fifteen-year sentence for armed robbery. He reported twice to his parole officer in San Francisco, and then disappeared. He's been on the wanted list ever since. We're going to have to verify his identity by checking dental charts, but the general description matches. The body isn't too badly decomposed. The climate here's so dry, it just kind of mummified."

"Poor Mr Thurgood," said Allie, in a nasty-nice voice. "I don't suppose he even knew the body was there."

"Of course he didn't know. He'd have called me right away if he'd known." The sheriff stood up to go. "Remember what I told you about that mine, young lady."

He and Uncle Harry went out and stood in the drive, talking quietly together.

"It *is* odd that Thurgood didn't explore his mine the moment he removed the grille from the entrance," said Jupe. "I certainly would if I purchased a mine."

"I told you he was a spook!" said Allie.

"Five years ago," said Jupiter. "Five years ago, in January, a thief named Gilbert Morgan was released from prison. He reported to his parole officer in San Francisco, then disappeared. Sometime between January and the time the mine was sealed in the spring, he came to Twin Lakes, got into the mine, and was killed. I wonder where he was in the meantime. Magdalena, could he have been here in town?"

Magdalena shook her head. "Twin Lakes is a small place. A stranger would be noticed."

Jupe nodded. "True. And if the man was a fugitive, he would not have wanted attention. He would have gone to a place where he could be part of a crowd and thus not be noticed. Yet he was here."

"I wonder what else happened in Twin Lakes

five years ago," said Allie. "The mine was sealed with the crook inside. Was anybody else in town who might be interesting? Like Wesley Thurgood, for instance?"

"I'd be very surprised if we found that he was." Bob had been leafing through a pile of newspapers that were stacked on the coffee table. "If it'll make you feel better, though, we can check."

"How?" asked Allie.

"The local paper," said Bob. He held up a tabloid-size sheet of newsprint. "The *Twin Lakes Gazette*. It has stories on absolutely everything that happens in town, including who is having guests and where the guests come from. If we could go through the files, we might find some clue in the back issues about what brought the crook named Gilbert Morgan to Twin Lakes."

"Great idea!" exclaimed Allie. "Let's go! I know the editor—he interviewed me when I came here. I'll keep him busy while you guys go through the back files."

"You think your uncle will let us out of the house?" asked Pete.

"I think he'll let us go anyplace," declared Allie, "so long as it isn't near that mine!"

7

Tracing the Dead Man

UNCLE HARRY FLATLY refused to permit Allie and the boys to leave the ranch that afternoon. Instead, he sent them out to prune Christmas trees until dinner-time. Allie sulked for hours.

By the next morning, however, Uncle Harry's mood had softened. When Allie told him she'd like to take The Three Investigators into town, he only said, "Don't be gone all day."

"We couldn't possibly be gone all day," Allie pointed out. "There isn't that much to Twin Lakes!"

Allie and the boys set out on foot for the mile-long hike down the dusty road. As they walked several cars passed them, going slowly up towards Thurgood's. One stopped as it came abreast of them and a man leaned out.

"This the road to Death Trap Mine?" called the man.

"Yes, it is," said Allie.

"Good!" The man started to drive on, then suddenly stopped again. "You wouldn't be the kids who found the body, would you?" he asked.

"Come on, Allie. Let's go." Bob took her arm and started to hurry her along.

"Hey, wait a second!" The man climbed out of his car with a camera in his hand. "Hey, I want to take your picture, okay?"

"No, it's not okay," said Pete.

The boys and Allie walked off as rapidly as they could without actually running. Another car passed them and they were aware of curious eyes staring at them.

"I guess it's to be expected," said Jupe. "The Death Trap Mine *did* make the news on television last night, and people *are* curious."

"But you'd better not pose for any pictures," Pete warned Allie. "I have a feeling your uncle wouldn't like it."

"I *know* he wouldn't like it," said Allie.

The main street in town was humming with activity. Cars cruised along and sightseers scanned the sidewalks. A little knot of men and women clustered outside the courthouse, where Sheriff Tait, looking red-faced and harassed, gestured as he talked with them.

"Reporters, following up on the story," said Bob.

The office of the *Twin Lakes Gazette* was in what had once been a store. A plate-glass window faced the street, and inside there were two battered desks. One was piled high with bills and notices, and newspapers from other parts of the West. At the second desk sat a string bean of a man with sparse, reddish hair and sharp features. He looked wildly excited, and he was pounding madly on a typewriter.

"Allie!" he shouted, when she came through the

56

door. "Just the girl I wanted to see! Been talkin'
to Ben Tait, and he tells me you're the one found
that body up at the mine."

Allie grinned. "Mr Kingsley, so far you're the
only one who's happy about it. Mr Thurgood
wants to knock my block off, Sheriff Tait says
he'll put me in jail if I ever go near the mine
again, and Uncle Harry's so mad at me . . ."

"I know. He'll get over it, don't you worry.
Only you'd better stay out of mines from now on.
Hate to have to write your obituary." The man
squinted at The Three Investigators. "These your
friends from Los Angeles?"

"Mr Kingsley, this is Jupiter Jones," said Allie.
"That's Pete Crenshaw over by the door, and Bob
Andrews is the one with the glasses—his dad
works for the *Los Angeles Times*."

"Well, now," said Kingsley. "That's some newspaper!"

"Yes, sir," Bob agreed. He was edging towards a
partition that separated the office from a huge dim
room in the back of the building. He could see a
small rotary press and a linotype machine. The
place was old and dusty, and smelled of printer's ink.

"Want to look around?" asked Kingsley.

"I'd like to very much," said Bob. "I'm interested in newspapers. Do you run the linotype yourself?"

"I do everything," Kingsley told him. "Most
weeks that doesn't amount to much. This week'll
be different. This week we've got news. Now Allie,
you just sit right there and tell me about looking
down that shaft and seeing that body, make your-

selves at home. Turn on the lights back there. Look at the press if you want."

The Three Investigators went back past the partition. Jupe touched a light switch and fluorescent fixtures in the ceiling filled the place with glare. Bob pointed to shelves along one wall. There were rows of file boxes, each one marked with dates.

"Those must be the old issues," Bob said.

"We want the ones for five years ago," murmured Jupe.

Bob nodded, and the three boys began to remove file boxes from the shelves. The papers for the year when the mine was sealed took up six file boxes.

"Go through every issue," said Jupe. "Scan the headlines. We don't want to miss anything that might possibly be a clue."

The three seated themselves on the floor, and each one opened a box, took out stacks of newspapers and began to work through them. They could hear Allie in the front office, her voice clear and excited, as she described to Kingsley what he doubtless already knew—that it was both thrilling and disturbing to find a dead body.

At first the old newspapers were disappointing. There were accounts of two small fires in the town. There was the report of the purchase of a new car by the sheriff's department. There were stories about visitors who had come to stay for a few days with relatives in Twin Lakes. There was nothing that could relate to Gilbert Morgan. But then, as he went through the issue for the week of 29th April, Jupe said, "This may be something."

"What is it?" asked Bob.

Jupe was silent for a minute, reading a news item to himself. Then he looked up. "A five-year-old girl wandered away from her home near town and was missing for three hours. She was found by a search party in Death Trap Mine. It seems that the entrance had once been boarded up, but over the years vandals and curiosity seekers had managed to remove some of the old boards. The little girl got into the mine and fell asleep. Her parents wanted to start a fund to raise money and have the mine sealed permanently. They said she could have been killed if she had gone further into the mine—and we know that indeed she could have."

Jupe looked around. "Where's the issue for May sixth?"

"Here," Bob held up a paper he had been reading. "There's a front-page story about the mine. The owner of the Twin Lakes Market put an empty five-gallon water jug next to his cash register and asked the citizens to donate to a fund for closing the mine. In two days they had raised enough for an iron grille to seal the mine entrance. The grille was ordered from Lordsburg, and they planned to seal the mine on May fourteenth."

There were further details about the planned sealing of the mine in the paper dated 13th May, and the issue for 20th May carried a story of the simple safety measure that had caused tremendous excitement in the little town. There had been a parade before the mine was sealed, then a ceremony as the grille was actually cemented into place.

"They made a big thing out of it," Pete observed.

"You heard what Mr Kingsley said," Bob reminded him. "There isn't much news here. Sealing the mine would be an event."

He turned the pages of the newspaper, looking at pictures of the residents of Twin Lakes parading down the village street. Suddenly he said, "Hey! Here's something. On the fourth page. When the people went out to put the grille in place at the mine entrance, they found a car abandoned on the mine property. It was a Chevrolet sedan, and it was identified as a car that had been stolen from the parking lot of a supermarket in Lordsburg three days before. Sheriff Tait is even quoted in the article. He guessed that the car had been swiped by Twin Lakes teenagers who wanted a ride home from Lordsburg. And he warned that if he caught any kids joyriding, he'd see to it that they wound up in jail."

Bob looked up. Jupe was pulling at his lower lip, as he often did when he was thinking intensely.

"A car stolen from Lordsburg, then found near the mine on the day the mine was sealed," he said. "And inside the mine was a convicted thief. I don't think we would be making a wild guess if we assumed that the car was stolen by the dead man. He drove it to Twin Lakes and left it near the mine. Then he went into the mine for some reason and . . . and he did not come out again."

"Okay," said Pete. "But that leaves us about where we were before, except that we can guess he went from San Francisco to Lordsburg and from Lordsburg to Twin Lakes. But why? What brought him here?"

Jupe shrugged.

Bob continued to look through old papers. There was nothing else that seemed remotely related to their mystery. Wesley Thurgood was not mentioned. In an issue for October of that year, Mrs Macomber's return to Twin Lakes was announced. Two follow-up stories told of her purchase of some of the property that had once belonged to Death Trap Mine.

"I wonder how long Gilbert Morgan was in Lordsburg after he left San Francisco?" said Jupiter.

Pete leaned against the linotype machine. "Who knows? He was a parole-breaker. He'd have laid low. And it all happened five years ago. The trail is cold by now."

"True," said Jupiter. "And he seems to have been here for no reason. Yet he was here, in a mine that was subsequently puchased by Wesley Thurgood. How could Thurgood not have known about that body? Could there be a connection between Thurgood, a successful real estate tycoon, and Morgan, a loser, a paroled convict? There is one thing we can do right now."

"What?" asked Pete.

"We can try to take a step backwards into Morgan's past. If he stayed in Lordsburg at all, he must have stayed somewhere. I know it's almost hopeless after all this time, but we can try to trace him. We can check the newspapers and old telephone directories. It's the only thing we *can* do."

8

A Prowler in the Night

ALLIE AND THE BOYS arrived back at the Christmas tree ranch in the early afternoon. Uncle Harry was standing on the porch, his ruddy face flushed with impatience. There were three cars in the drive, and several people were clustered near the porch, trying to argue with Uncle Harry.

"My niece cannot possibly talk with anyone," Uncle Harry was saying. "She's a sensitive young girl, and she's far too upset after . . ."

He broke off short when he saw Allie and the boys. "Allie—into the house!" He jumped off the porch, took Allie by the elbow, and propelled her through the door. Jupiter, Pete, and Bob hurried after her, and when they were inside, Uncle Harry slammed the door behind them.

"Those people are reporters and I do not want you talking to them," said Uncle Harry.

"Why not?" asked Allie. "I'm news, aren't I?"

"Because if your mother should find out what you've been up to, she'd have my head, that's why not," said Uncle Harry.

"Well, it's too late to worry about newspapers," said Allie. "I just talked to Mr Kingsley."

"Kingsley's different," Uncle Harry said. "Your

folks aren't likely to pick up a copy of the *Twin Lakes Gazette* anywhere in the Far East. Now I want you to stay inside for the rest of today. You, too, boys. And stick close by tomorrow, too, if those people are still around."

"Mr Osborne," said Jupe, "we had hoped to go to Lordsburg tomorrow."

"What for?" asked Uncle Harry.

Jupe put his hand into his pocket and took out the pebble he had found in the mine. "I wanted to show this to a jeweller. It's the pebble I found yesterday in Death Trap Mine."

Harrison Osborne smiled. "I suppose you think it's a gold nugget. Well, it isn't. There's no gold here. But I do have to go into Lordsburg later this week. You and Allie can come with me. As a matter of fact all of you can come along. I wouldn't think of leaving you at home. I'm afraid of what you'd get up to."

Uncle Harry went outside to get rid of the reporters. The Three Investigators and Allie spent the rest of the day reading and playing Monopoly. From time to time Allie ran upstairs to stand on the landing outside the bunkroom and look out towards Wesley Thurgood's property. She reported gleefully that Thurgood was standing guard over his domain with a shotgun, and that the dog, exhausted with barking at curiosity seekers, had stretched out and gone to sleep.

That evening the boys went up to the bunkroom early. From their windows they could see a light on in Thurgood's cabin. But even before they got into bed, Thurgood put out his light.

Soon the lights went out in Mrs Macomber's house across the road.

"Guess everybody's tired tonight," said Pete. He rolled into his bunk. "I know I am, but I'm darned if I know why."

"Some kind of delayed reaction," said Bob. "It was spooky, seeing that guy in the mine yesterday. I know he was a crook and all, but that was a nasty way to go."

"I wonder what he was doing here," said Jupe aloud. He had wondered it to himself many times that day. "Perhaps we'll find some trace of him in Lordsburg."

"You really going to show that pebble to a jeweller?" asked Bob.

"It can't hurt," said Jupiter, "and it will give us an excuse to go off by ourselves while we're there. I'm sure Uncle Harry doesn't want us to concern ourselves with the dead hold-up man in any way—but we *are* concerned."

"Allie isn't," said Bob as he put out the light. "She's just concerned with Wesley Thurgood, and I don't think we're going to find any connection between Thurgood and the crook."

"Maybe not, but I'm bothered by the fact that Thurgood didn't find the body himself," Jupe replied. "He wasn't even curious enough to explore his own mine, which is very strange indeed."

The boys dozed off, each thinking of the man in the mine, each wondering how he had come to be there and exactly how he had met his death.

It was very late when Pete woke up. He frowned in the darkness and listened intently. Something had moved outside, beyond the open windows. He lifted himself on one elbow when the sound came to him again—a lurching, sticky squeak.

"Jupe!" He kept his voice low. "Bob! Listen!"

"Huh?" Bob turned over. "What is it?"

"Someone just opened the barn door." Pete was up and crossing to the window in his bare feet. He leaned on the window-sill and looked out. Bob and Jupe joined him.

"The door's closed now," said Bob.

Then the boys saw a light moving inside the barn, dancing on the dusty, side windows of the place. The light flickered and went out, and then flared up again.

"Someone's lighting matches!" said Jupe. "Come on."

It took only seconds for the Investigators to pull on shirts and jeans and stick their bare feet into sandshoes. They crept down the stairs and opened the front door without a sound.

The moon had set when they came out on to the drive. They groped towards the barn with Jupe in the lead. They had almost reached the barn when Bob put his foot down on a rock in the drive, turned his ankle, and let out a barely audible cry as he crumpled to the ground.

The light in the barn had flickered again. Now the barn went dark.

"Blast!" breathed Pete.

Bob sat on the ground rubbing his ankle and looking towards the barn. After a moment he got up and the three boys again crept towards the old building. Jupe put his hand out and touched the door-latch, which rattled slightly.

Suddenly the barn door swung out, catching Jupe in the chest and knocking him to the ground. Pete leaped to one side as a burly figure dashed into the open, pounded past them, and disappeared among the Christmas trees beside the drive.

"What's that?" came a roar from the house. "Who's out there?"

Jupe picked himself up. "There was a prowler in the barn," he called.

"Oh, good grief!" said Uncle Harry, "I'll call the sheriff."

Pete pointed towards Thurgood's place. "He went that way."

The boys listened, but there was no sound. The fields of trees were dark and still. "He can't be far," said Jupe.

Pete swallowed and slowly stepped in among the trees. He strained his ears, listening for some sound, alert for some movement in the fields. For a few minutes he was aware of Bob and Jupe coming up behind him. Then Jupe went off quietly to the left and Bob slipped away towards the right. Pete crept forward alone, one careful footstep after another, avoiding the tree branches that might catch at his legs.

Then Pete stopped. He could hear the blood rushing in his own ears, and he could hear something else—a gasping, rasping sound; the sound of laboured breathing. Someone was quite close to him, fighting for breath as if he had been running for a long distance.

Pete froze where he was, listening, and the

harsh breathing went on. The unknown person seemed to be only a few feet from Pete, just beyond an evergreen that Pete could touch with his hands. Pete opened his mouth to call out for Jupe and Bob, then hesitated. His cry would only send the prowler off again.

When Pete heard a car on the road from town, he grinned. That would be the sheriff coming in answer to Uncle Harry's call—and Pete had the intruder pinned down.

But as the car turned in at the gate and the headlights swept across the fields, the prowler dashed from the shelter of a bushy tree. Pete leaped after him. But then he saw, against the night sky, an upraised arm—and something that made him throw himself to the ground. As he went down a murderous blade flashed through the air, slicing the top off a small tree! Then the stranger was gone again, gasping and stumbling as he crashed off across the fields.

Pete got to his knees, shaking.

Jupe was suddenly beside him.

"A machete!" said Pete. "He had a machete! And he almost took my head off!"

9

The Earth Rumbles

SHERIFF TAIT HAD A deputy with him—a young man named Blythe. When the two men heard of the intruder in the barn, and of his slashing attack with the machete, they took powerful flashlights and started across the fields. They picked up the trail of the prowler next to the tree where Pete had been standing. Footprints went away from the tree, and the sheriff followed them until they were lost among a jumble of prints on the road near Thurgood's place.

The boys and Allie watched from the upstairs windows of the ranch house. The sheriff and his deputy continued to search. They roused Thurgood and entered his cabin while his guard dog barked ferociously. They went into the mine. Mrs Macomber was up and her lights were on. They went into her house and then into each of the abandoned houses she owned. More than an hour later they returned to the ranch house.

"Whoever it was," the sheriff told Uncle Harry, "he must have gone up the mountainside. We'll never trail him up there in the dark. Not much point, anyway. It's probably one of those weirdos who came from Lordsburg or Silver City when they heard about the body in the mine. You get crackpots whenever anything unusual happens. But I wish he hadn't panicked and taken that machete."

Sheriff Tait and Deputy Blythe went back to town, and Uncle Harry locked the front door and closed all the windows on the ground floor.

In the morning, the boys were wakened by hearty laughter from below. They went down to find Allie perched on a stool in the kitchen, watching with obvious pleasure as Mrs Macomber sat at the table, drinking coffee and talking with great animation to Magdalena. The widow's tanned face was alive with excitement.

"Sorry if we disturbed you last night," said Jupe, when he and the others had been introduced.

"I'm not." Mrs Macomber laughed. "It reminded me of the old days. Forty-five years ago Twin Lakes was quite a town! The sheriff had to break up fights every Saturday night."

"Say," said Allie, "speaking of the old days, do you remember Wesley Thurgood?"

Mrs Macomber laughed. "How could I forget him? I see him every day."

"No," said Allie. "I mean, do you remember when he was a little kid? He says he was born here."

"And so he was," said Mrs Macomber. "His folks lived in the little green house down by the court-house and his father was foreman on the night shift. He was a real mining man. Wesley was the last boy born in town before I left here. That was at the end of the boom days and people had started to move away. Wesley was only a toddler when the mine shut down and he and his folks left. I keep meaning to ask him about his parents—what they did after they left Twin Lakes—but I never get a chance. He's so darned busy driving around in that fancy red truck of his, lugging stuff in, pottering around the mine. He was out at dawn this morning. I saw him go by wearing that ridiculous hard hat, which he needs the way I need another head."

The group in the kitchen heard a car pass by on the road. Allie ran upstairs to the window on the landing. She was back shortly with the news that Thurgood had returned and that he had two men with him. "They looked like Mexicans," she reported. "Now what's he up to?"

"Why don't you ask him?" prompted Mrs Macomber.

"Because he isn't speaking to me," said Allie, "and if I bother him again, Uncle Harry swore he'd lock me up."

"I doubt that," Mrs Macomber told her. She took her leave and returned to her own house across the road.

In the days that followed The Three Investigators finished pruning the largest field of Christmas trees and started work on another. Allie pruned, too, but she also spent a great deal of time riding Queenie in the field near Wesley Thurgood's place. She saw that the two dark-haired, dark-eyed labourers seemed to be living in the big building that had once housed the mine works. A shiny new padlock had been put on a little wooden shed that stood near the mine entrance. Thurgood continued to drive out on his mysterious errands. The second day after the labourers arrived, a truck delivered sacks of cement, dozens of steel fence posts, and great rolls of chain-link fencing. Under Thurgood's direction, the two men set to work putting up an eight-foot fence around Thurgood's property.

At lunch that day, Allie said, "He's going to a lot of trouble to protect a worthless mine. Who cares about the mine, anyway?"

"You do," said her uncle. "You'd give your eye-teeth to get in there and he knows it. To say nothing of those creeps who came swarming in when that body was found. I don't blame him for fencing his place. If people were as interested in Christmas trees as they are in mines, I'd fence this property."

Uncle Harry left after lunch to spray weeds in the field near the road. Jupe leaned back in his chair and frowned. "No one *is* interested in Christmas trees," he said. "So why was there a prowler in the barn the other night? What is there in the barn that would interest even the most avid curiosity seeker?"

The others couldn't answer him. When the dishes had been cleared away they all trooped out to the barn to look around again.

"Nothing," said Pete. "A lot of hay for the horses, some tools and hoses, and an old car that doesn't run."

"Maybe the prowler just wanted a machete," said Allie.

"That's a gruesome idea," said Bob. "A machete is an ugly weapon. And if someone wanted a weapon, why a machete? A gun would be better and lots of people around here must have guns."

They left the barn in time to see Thurgood's red Chevy Suburban pass the gate. It was headed towards the mine. A man sat in the front seat with Thurgood—a dignified-looking gentleman who wore a light summer suit and a white hat. Allie and the boys raced into the ranch-house and up to the landing outside the bunkroom, where they could have a better view of Thurgood's property and his visitor.

The two labourers were not working on the fence. Instead, the watchers saw one of them emerge from the mine. He was staring straight ahead in a stolid manner as he pushed a wheelbarrow loaded with dirt and rocks. He came abreast of Thurgood and his companion. Thurgood stopped him, picked a handful of earth out of the barrow, and showed it to his guest. Then he spoke to the labourer, who went on with the wheelbarrow, trundled it up a ramp made of two stout planks, and disappeared through an open door in the side of the big mine works. Thurgood and his visitor went into the mine.

A minute later Allie and the boys heard the sound of a muffled explosion. It rumbled on for a few seconds and then died away.

"He's shooting again!" cried Allie.

"That didn't sound like a gun," said Jupiter. "It sounded like something much more powerful. An explosive of some kind!"

73

Across the road, Mrs Macomber came out on her porch and looked towards the mine.

Thurgood and his visitor appeared in the mine entrance. They were accompanied by the second labourer. He, too, trudged into the mine works pushing a loaded wheelbarrow. Thurgood and his guest stood in the clearing talking for a few minutes. Then they got into the red truck and Thurgood drove down the road. He ignored Mrs Macomber, who was still on her porch. When he had gone, she crossed the road and came up Uncle Harry's drive, trying impatiently to reclasp a large Indian bracelet.

The Three Investigators and Allie went downstairs and met Mrs Macomber at the door. "How about that?" she cried. "Wesley Thurgood is working the mine!"

Magdalena came out of the kitchen. "But no, Senora Macomber!" she protested. "In that mine there is nothing. You have said so yourself. All of the silver is gone."

"But he's working it anyway," insisted Mrs Macomber. "He's blasting. Didn't you hear it? I couldn't be mistaken about that sound. I've heard it too many times."

"He's playing games," said Pete. "Or maybe he's going to make the mine into a tourist attraction. You know, like the people who buy old ghost towns and fix them up."

Mrs Macomber looked upset. "He'll ruin the place! Tourists mean traffic jams and litter."

"Well it *is* his property," said Allie, mimicking her uncle.

Mrs Macomber made an impatient noise and walked out. Jupe rocked on his heels, considering the situation. "I doubt that Wesley Thurgood is going to open the mine to tourists," he decided. "Twin Lakes is too far off the beaten track."

"Then what is he doing?" demanded Pete.

Jupe smiled. "We could try asking his Mexican labourers," he said. "Thurgood and his guest are gone. Let's go up and see what the men have to say."

A few minutes later The Three Investigators and Allie stood by the fence around Thurgood's property and called to the two men. They tried addressing them in English and got no answer. They tried a few words of Spanish, but that brought no reply either. The two Mexicans simply eyed them suspiciously.

Frustrated, they returned to the house to enlist Magdalena's help.

"You speak their language, Magdalena," said Pete. "They'd trust you, don't you think?"

Magdalena went towards Thurgood's place willingly enough, but she was soon back to report failure. The men had ignored her. She had got close enough, before the dog saw her and barked, to overhear them talking quietly together, but she had caught only one word: *oro*.

"Oro?" echoed Jupe. "That means gold! Could Thurgood be working the mine for gold?"

"But it is a silver mine!" protested Magdalena.

"Gold and silver are often found near each other," said Jupe. He took out the pebble with the odd little shiny streak. "Allie, when did your uncle say he was going into Lordsburg?"

"He's going tomorrow," reported Allie.

"And we're going with him. We'll see exactly what's in this pebble."

10

Is the Glitter Gold?

UNCLE HARRY PARKED the station wagon beside the express office in Lordsburg. "I ordered three loads of young trees from San Jose," he said. "After I pick them up I have to go to the builder's supply company for some things I need. I'll meet you boys back here at one o'clock, and we'll have some lunch before we start back to the ranch."

"I'm going with Jupe and Pete and Bob," Allie announced.

"Okay. Just stay out of trouble," said Uncle Harry. "Though I don't know why I should worry. There's no mine here for you to get into."

He left them and went into the express office.

"What's first?" demanded Allie eagerly.

"We check out Jupe's pebble, huh?" said Pete. "That shouldn't take long. Do we tell the jeweller where we found it when we show it to him?"

"I think not," said Jupiter. "We don't want any more prowlers, and if the streak in the pebble *is* gold, that might bring them swarming. Leave it to me. I'll think of something to say."

Two blocks from the express office they found a small shop with a display of watches and pendants in the window. A sign indicated that the proprietor, J. B. Atkinson, bought old gold and silver.

"Exactly what we need." Jupiter Jones opened the door and they went in.

A plump, rosy-faced man sat on a stool behind a glass partition. He had a jeweller's lens in one eye and was repairing a watch. They saw a case with some worn but beautiful silver pieces on display and several handsome old gold pins and rings.

"Mr Atkinson?" said Jupiter.

The man behind the partition put down a tiny screwdriver, took the lens from his eye, and smiled.

Jupe took out his pebble. "We've been staying with friends near Silver City," he told the man. "We were out hiking in the hills yesterday, and we met an old prospector."

Atkinson nodded. "There are still some around."

"He said he needed money," Jupiter went on. "He said he'd been carrying this for a long time, but he'd sell it to us." Jupe handed the pebble to Atkinson.

Atkinson looked at the pebble, squinted, and rubbed it with his finger. His smile did not change. "How much did you pay for it?" he asked.

"Five dollars," said Jupiter.

"Is it real?" asked Allie.

"It's a real pebble, right enough," said Atkinson. "Whether the stuff in it is gold or not, we'll see. He opened a drawer and took out a small bottle of liquid and a little file. He cut a tiny notch in the shiny streak of the pebble with the file, then put a drop of the liquid on to the notch. "This stuff is nitric acid," he said. "'Most any metal *except* gold will react with it." After a moment he nodded. "Yep. I'd say you've got gold here."

"Does pure gold often exist in nature?" asked Jupe.

"It's usually combined with other metals," said the jeweller. "This looks to be pretty fine stuff. Wonder where your prospector pal got it."

"He didn't say," Jupe replied.

"I doubt if it matters." Atkinson handed the pebble back to Jupe. "I'd guess it's from some worked-out mine, probably in California. Prospectors can still make enough to keep themselves in beans by panning the streams near the old mines."

Jupe put the pebble in his pocket. "You say gold is usually combined with other metals. Do you think there's any silver in this gold?" he asked.

"No. it's reddish, which might mean some copper. Silver gives gold a greenish colour." He opened one of the cases and took out a pin which looked very old. It was made of gold which had a greenish cast, and it was formed in the shape of a leaf. "This is what we call green gold. It's about twenty-five per cent silver, which means it's eighteen-carat gold. Those little finger rings there in the case are even finer. They're baby rings. People used to buy them for children for christening presents. They're more than twenty-carat gold, and that's why some of them are worn through. They're quite soft. I sell one now and then, just as a curiosity. And that's what you've got there in your pebble. A curiosity. A hunk of the old gold rush days."

"Worth five dollars?" asked Pete.

"I reckon so," said Atkinson. "You pay can more than that for a hunk of something plastic these days. Hang on to it. If you ever feel like having it made into a tie clasp or anything, come back and see me."

They thanked him and went out to the street.

"The real McCoy!" exclaimed Pete. "There's gold in that mine!"

"And copper, too," said Jupe thoughtfully. "But the gold in our pebble isn't mixed with silver. Odd, since Death Trap Mine was a silver mine in the old days. I know that gold and silver can often be found in the same mine, but gold and silver *and* copper!"

"Interesting, isn't it?" said Allie. "That creep Thurgood has found a vein of ore that nobody even suspected was there. His father worked in the mine. Maybe his father knew something and told it to Thurgood. So Thurgood made up that cockeyed story about how he wanted to return to his old hometown, and he bought the Death Trap and now he's working it."

Jupe frowned. "If that's true—that there was a family legend about a secret vein of gold—then why would Thurgood wait so long to come here? He's at least forty. He could have investigated the mine anytime in the last twenty years, and bought it cheaply. Maybe he had no interest in it when he was a young man, but he should have had some interest a few years ago, when the price of gold went up. Why didn't Thurgood show up then?"

"How do we know he didn't?" Allie insisted.

"How do we know he wasn't here five years ago, when Gilbert Morgan fell down the shaft? Maybe they were confederates. Maybe they got to fighting and Thurgood shoved Morgan."

"Allie, that's wild!" protested Bob. "Why should a super-successful real estate man get all heated up about an old mine? There wouldn't be any reason. And if there is gold and he knew it, he wouldn't need a confederate. Nobody asked any questions when he just bought the property, did they? But speaking of that crook . . . hadn't we better start tracing him?"

Bob took out his notebook and read: "Gilbert Morgan, parole violator. Also used the names George Milling, Glenn Mercer, and George Martins. Released from San Quentin and disappeared from San Francisco five years ago. Probably left San Francisco late in January or early in February. Probably reached Twin Lakes sometime in May of that year, using a car stolen in Lordsburg."

"A good summary, Records," said Jupiter.

"He always used the initials G. M., no matter what his alias," said Bob. "That is all we have to go on. If he was in Lordsburg for any length of time, he may have left some trace. Shall we try the public library?" he asked. "They'll have phone books, city directories, and back issues of the local newspaper."

Allie led the way to the library, where a librarian listened to Jupe explain that he was vacationing in the area and was trying to locate a long-lost uncle. "He sent my mother a postcard from Lordsburg five years ago," said Jupe. "We wrote to him, but the letters came back because we didn't have a real address. I promised my mother I'd try to find him."

The librarian, impressed by Jupe's earnest manner, produced telephone books and city directories for the last five years. Allie and the boys sat at a long table and started checking the five-year-old directories. "Look for a name with the initials G. M.," said Jupe. "A name that only appears in one directory or one telephone book—the one for five years ago."

It did not take long. In ten minutes they had checked the names of sixteen persons with the initials G. M. against the directories for the following year. All but one had remained in Lordsburg. The one odd name, Gilbert Maynard, was missing from several directories, but appeared in the current telephone book. "He must be someone who moved away and then returned," said Jupe. "He took up residence at the same address."

"So he can't be our crook," said Pete. "Okay. Morgan passed through town without doing any of the ordinary things, like having a telephone or a job, or getting himself listed as a resident."

"He was only here a few months, if he stayed at all," Bob pointed out.

"Any luck?" called the librarian.

"No. No, it looks as if my uncle didn't stay here," confessed Jupe. He then managed to look very much embarrassed. "Uncle Geoffrey did have a way of . . . ah . . . attracting attention. Maybe the newspapers for that year . . . ?"

"Oh, he was that sort, was he?" The librarian shook her head, but she showed the way to the room where periodicals were on file, and left them to go through bound volumes of the Lordsburg newspapers. There was nothing—nothing that could be remotely connected with the deceased hold-up man—until they came to the issue for 10th May, five years before. "Death Trap Mine to Be Sealed," Bob read from a headline. "So it *was* announced in the paper here in Lordsburg. Could that have had anything to do with our guy's death?"

Jupe shrugged. "Who knows? He could have seen the story in the paper and decided for some reason to go to Twin Lakes and explore the mine. What day was the car stolen from the supermarket parking lot?"

Bob consulted his notes. "May eleventh," he said. "That's one day after the sealing of the mine was announced in the Lordsburg newspaper and three days before the mine actually was closed up. There could be a connection."

"But what, for Pete's sake?" cried Allie. "The crook sees the story about the mine being sealed and he's in such a sweat to get there that he swipes a car and drives it to Twin Lakes, where he dashes into the mine, falls down a shaft, breaks his neck, and is not heard of again for five years! That doesn't make sense. Now suppose he and Thurgood had a meeting set up . . ."

"Allie!" snapped Pete. "Can't you forget about Wesley Thurgood for just a minute?"

"We're about where we started," said Bob. "We know that Gilbert Morgan could have been in Lordsburg and he could have stolen a car and driven to Twin Lakes, but we can't prove it. It was a long chance, but we had to check it out."

"The morning isn't completely wasted," said Jupiter. "We are sure of one thing." He took out his pebble. "We know that there was at least this much gold in Death Trap Mine on the day Morgan's body was found. I'm not sure how much that means, but I'm sure it means something!"

II

The Hungry Thief

IT WAS MID-AFTERNOON when they arrived back at the Christmas tree ranch. The boys helped Uncle Harry unload the station wagon, putting the loads of tiny trees out near the barn and watering them with a hose. When Uncle Harry went into the house, Jupe looked across at Mrs Macomber's place.

"I imagine your neighbour knows more about the Death Trap Mine than almost anyone in town," said Jupe.

"Mrs Macomber? She sure does," said Allie.

"Let's pay her a call," Jupe suggested.

The others were more than willing. They went down the drive and across the road and knocked on Mrs Macomber's door. The widow called to them to come in. Allie opened the door and they walked directly into the neat little kitchen.

"Busy?" Allie asked Mrs Macomber.

She smiled, and the wrinkles at the corners of her eyes deepened. "Don't have all that much to be busy about these days," she said. "But I sure would appreciate it if one of you boys would step out to my truck and bring in the carton that's in the back. I've got to put away my groceries in the fridge or the frozen stuff will melt."

"I'll do it," said Pete. Mrs Macomber's small pick-up truck stood in a dirt driveway beside the house. There was a large cardboard carton jammed with brown paper bags in the back of the truck. Pete brought it into the kitchen and put it down on a counter.

"Much obliged," said Mrs Macomber. "I just can't seem to do all the things I used to," She began to take out vegetables, bread, and packages of frozen foods and pile them on the counter.

Suddenly there was a dull booming sound. Mrs Macomber went to a window. "Wesley Thurgood's playing miner again," she announced. "I've been kind of expecting that. I saw him drive in half an hour ago with one of his city visitors."

"He seems to be actually working the mine," said Jupiter.

"Sounds that way," agreed Mrs Macomber. "He's setting off explosives in the mine, that's for sure. I was born here and I know that sound. I lived in this very house when my husband was superintendent here. You can't mistake dynamite going off in a mine tunnel. But Thurgood isn't working the mine full-time. He does his blasting only when he's got company. Showing off for his rich friends from Los Angeles, I suppose."

"It's a weird hobby," said Bob.

"I've known of stranger ones." Mrs Macomber smiled. "I once heard of a man who bought an old railroad locomotive. He had three hundred yards of track put down in a field behind his house and he ran his locomotive back and forth on that. He wore a conductor's uniform whenever he played with his big toy, and he had a ball. Lots of money'll do that to folks. Maybe Wesley Thurgood's got some fuzzy notions of the old days when his dad was a miner, and he's trying to go back to that time. It's harmless."

"You make him sound so innocent," said Allie.

"Take my advice and don't complicate things if you don't have to," warned Mrs Macomber. "The truth of the matter is—you've got it in for Thurgood because he's sore at you. I don't suppose I blame you. He isn't very friendly and I'm glad he's finally got a fence around his place. I didn't like that dog of his running loose. But then, I don't have the right to tell him how chatty he's supposed to be or what kind of a dog he can own."

The booming sounded again from the mine.

"Mrs Macomber," said Jupe, "is there any possibility that Thurgood is working the mine for profit?"

She shook her head. "The Death Trap Mine is dead, dead, dead. The silver was played out forty years ago. I ought to know. My husband and I had a rough time after the mine closed. We had to leave here. You think we'd have gone if there was any chance of staying? Then after Henry died—he had a heart attack twenty-two years back—I took the insurance money and opened a shop in Phoenix. Sold Indian jewellery and moccasins to the tourists, but I lost everything. I'm no businesswoman. I had to sell out and I wound up working in the same place I'd owned, scraping and saving and standing on my feet all day." Her expression had become bleak. Suddenly her look softened. "I wanted to retire here," she went on. "I wanted to get back to the place where I'd been happy, and I'm glad I did. Maybe that's what Thurgood wants. I remember when he was a dirty-faced kid, toddling around Twin Lakes licking a lollipop. There was something peculiar about that boy even then . . . but I just can't remember . . ."

"But the mine . . ." insisted Allie.

"Well, the mine made Twin Lakes what it was," said Mrs Macomber. "But I don't feel I have to own it to bring back the good memories. Maybe Wesley Thurgood does. Maybe he's got to play the role all the way and really be a miner, like his father."

"And there's no chance he's taking anything out of the mine?" Jupe persisted.

"No chance. There's nothing left to take."

"Even if the silver is gone," said Jupe, "could there be gold? Silver and gold are often found together."

"Not at Death Trap."

"Copper?" suggested Jupe.

"No. There was silver and the silver is gone." She shook herself, as if to get rid of an unpleasant thought. "Now that's enough of that. When the mine was open Twin Lakes was a boom town and we had some good times. And today I own a hunk of what used to be that boom town. If we ever have another wave of prosperity around here, I can fix up my five houses and rent them and make a fortune in my old age. C'mon. I'll show you boys my little estate."

Mrs Macomber led Allie and the boys outside. "I thought about putting padlocks on the doors when I moved in here," she said. "But I'd have to put a trail of silver dollars from the highway to this place to get even a hobo up here—or at least I felt that way until Allie found the hold-up man in the mine. There were plenty of strangers around here after that. Did they ever find your uncle's missing machete, Allie?"

"No, they didn't," said Allie.

"It'll probably turn up all rusty someplace on the mountain," said Mrs Macomber. She walked to an old frame house that stood to the north of her own residence. "This place belonged to the McKestries," she told them. "He was a paymaster at the mine."

Mrs Macomber pushed on the door and it opened with squealing protest. Allie and the boys followed her inside. They saw long-unused furnishings, cracked plaster, and cupboards with doors that sagged open to show odd pieces of chipped pottery. "Lots of people left things behind," said Mrs Macomber. "I guess they figured some stuff wasn't worth taking."

"You'd have to do a lot of clearing out and fixing up before you could rent this place," Allie told her.

"Of course I would. I had to do a lot to my house before I could move back into it. But it was fun."

As they went from one place to another in Mrs Macomber's domain they sniffed air that was heavy with dust and dry rot. In some of the houses the roofs had let in the rain, and ceilings were splotched and stained. In one, a heap of yellowed newspapers was piled near a rusted wood-burning stove.

Bob crouched and flipped through the old newspapers. "Were these here when you bought your property, Mrs Macomber?" he asked. "I mean, when you came back five years ago?"

"I suppose so," said Mrs Macomber. "Well, of course, they must have been. How else would they get here?"

"Interesting," said Bob. "Could I have them?"

"What on earth do you want with a pile of old newspapers?" asked Mrs Macomber

"He's a newspaper nut!" Allie laughed "But he sure helped us find out a lot about what was going on here five years ago. After we discovered that body in the mine, we went down to the *Twin Lakes Gazette* to see if we could figure out what Gilbert Morgan might have been doing here. We found out a whole bunch of stuff, but—"

Jupe shot Allie a menacing glance as Bob interrupted her. "My dad's a newspaperman," said Bob. "He's got me interested in old papers. Could I take these?"

Mrs Macomber seemed puzzled for a moment. "Well, I guess you can have them," she said.

Bob carefully picked up the stack of newspapers and held them at his side, and they all went out into the late-afternoon sun.

"Say, would you kids like something to drink or will that spoil your dinner?" Mrs Macomber asked.

"*Nothing* can spoil Jupe's dinner!" Allie laughed.

"Good, I've got some orange soda."

They returned to Mrs Macomber's snug little house, but there was no soda in the refrigerator or in the cupboard or in the pantry that opened off the kitchen. "What on earth?" Mrs Macomber exclaimed. "I'm sure I had some orange soda. I know I didn't drink it all myself."

Jupe, with his eye for detail, stared at the groceries still piled on the counter. "You also had a loaf of bread," he said. "And some canned tuna. They're gone!"

Mrs Macomber looked at Jupe as though she didn't understand. Then she gasped. She charged out on to the porch and peered up and down the road, as if expecting to see someone walking off with her supplies.

Bob put down his newspapers. He removed a soggy cigarette butt from the gleaming kitchen sink and held it up between two fingers. "Mrs Macomber," he said "You don't smoke, do you?"

Mrs Macomber stared at Bob's find.

"No, I certainly don't," she said. By now Mrs Macomber seemed to have recovered from her shock. "I can't understand why anyone would steal from me," she said. "If someone wanted some food, all he had to do was ask me!"

"Well, he didn't," said Pete. "Maybe he wanted more than food. We'd better check the rest of the house."

Mrs Macomber shrugged and led the way out of the kitchen. They went through every room and closet of the immaculate little house. No intruder lurked under the furniture, and not one of the widow's many knick-knacks and mementoes seemed out of position.

"I don't have any valuables," said Mrs Macomber. "And nothing else is missing."

"I suggest you get those padlocks after all, Mrs Macomber," said Jupiter. "And lock this house when you go out."

"But no one around here locks up," protested Mrs Macomber.

"There have been strangers around lately," Jupe pointed out. "Morbid people drawn here by the finding of the hold-up man's body in the mine. If one of them helped himself to your food—he might just come back!"

12

A New Suspect

A FEW MINUTES LATER The Three Investigators and
Allie crossed the road to Harrison Osborne's property. Bob was lugging his stack of newspapers.

"What's with those?" Pete asked, indicating the
papers. "They of great historical interest or something?"

"And why did you guys shut me up back there?"
said Allie.

Bob shifted the pile of papers so that his companions could see the one on top. "Most of these
are copies of the *Twin Lakes Gazette*," he said.
"They're more than forty years old. They must
have been left in the house by whoever lived there
before the mine closed. But the paper on top is a
Phoenix paper, and the date is five years ago—May
ninth. Look at that headline!"

"Hm!" said Jupiter. "I suggest that we find a
private place and read that article with care."

The Three Investigators and Allie hurried past
Uncle Harry's house and into the barn, where Bob
put the papers down in a pile near the old Model T.
They knelt on the floor and Bob unfolded the
Phoenix newspaper with its bold headline.

ARMOURED CAR HELD UP
MASKED MEN ESCAPE WITH $250,000!

Today at 3 P.M. an armoured truck belonging to the Securities Transport Corporation was robbed outside the Phoenician Savings and Loan Company on North Indian Head Road. Three men wearing ski masks and armed with sawn-off shotguns forced driver Thomas Serrano and guard Joseph Ardmore into the rear of their truck. After binding and gagging Serrano and Ardmore, the hold-up men escaped with an undisclosed amount in negotiable securities, and cash estimated at approximately $250,000.

According to a witness who asked that his name be withheld, the thieves got into a white Chrysler sedan that was parked near the armoured truck. They crouched on the floor. A woman then emerged from a nearby card shop, took the wheel of the Chrysler, and sped away from the bank, heading north on Indian Head Road. No complete description of the hold-up men could be obtained, but the woman was described as between 55 and 60 years of age, slender, with slightly greying hair and tanned skin. She is said to be approximately 5 feet 7 inches tall, weighs about 130 pounds and was clad in dark slacks and a white turtleneck shirt. The witness reported that she wore an unusually large Indian necklace of turquoise and silver.

"Wow!" said Pete. "They got a quarter of a million bucks!"

Jupe mused, "May ninth. That paper is five years old and it's dated May ninth. Bob, wasn't that the day before the sealing of Death Trap Mine was announced in the Lordsburg newspaper?"

"Right," said Bob. "And on May eleventh, five years ago, a car was stolen from Lordsburg."

"At that time," said Jupiter, "all of Mrs Macomber's houses were empty—she didn't come back to Twin Lakes and purchase her property until October. But *someone* who had been in Phoenix on May ninth was here and left that paper in one of the houses that she now owns."

"Gilbert Morgan, the dead hold-up guy!" cried Pete.

"It seems possible," agreed Jupe. "Phoenix is not far from Lordsburg. A quarter of a million dollars stolen only days before Death Trap Mine was sealed. . . . Then a car stolen in Lordsburg and driven to Twin Lakes, and five years later the body of a known hold-up man is found in the closed mine. . . . Yes, it's conceivable that Morgan was in Phoenix on the ninth of May—holding up an armoured car—and that he went immediately to Lordsburg and then came to Twin Lakes. And I think we can figure out what he was doing here."

"He was hiding out!" declared Pete.

"No," said Jupiter. "No one would hide out in a place like Twin Lakes. A stranger in this town would be too obvious. But suppose that Morgan took part in that robbery and was looking for a safe place to hide his share of the loot. What could be safer than a mine that was about to be sealed?"

Allie looked bewildered. "But if he put it in a sealed mine, how would he get it out again?"

"I don't think a little iron grille would be much problem for a determined crook," Bob pointed out.

"Then Thurgood's got the dough!" cried Allie. "If it was hidden in the mine, Thurgood's got it! No wonder he didn't let on that the body was there. He probably planned to get rid of it so no one could ever guess he found the money. But we got there first!"

"That is possible," said Jupiter. "But let's not worry about who has the loot just yet. There's another reason why Gilbert Morgan might have chosen to come to Twin Lakes."

"What's that?" asked Bob.

"Suppose that Gilbert Morgan knew more about Death Trap Mine than what he read in the Lordsburg newspaper. Suppose he knew someone who told him all about the played-out mine—and the abandoned mine property. Suppose that person was one of his accomplices!"

"What are you getting at?" demanded Allie.

"After years of working in a little shop in Phoenix, Mrs Macomber returned to Twin Lakes —several months after the robbery. She had enough money to buy a sizeable piece of property. Perhaps *she* was an accomplice of Morgan's!"

"You're nuts!" cried Allie.

"Oh, I don't think so," said Jupe airily. "Records, give us that description of the driver of the getaway car again."

"Golly!" exclaimed Bob. "It was a woman, between fifty-five and sixty years of age, with slightly greying hair and tanned skin. Approximately five feet seven inches tall, and weighing about a hundred and thirty pounds. And she was wearing Indian jewellery!"

"Does that sound like anyone we know?" asked Jupiter.

"But . . . but there must be millions of people who look like that," Allie declared. "And Mrs Macomber's such a nice lady."

"Nice is not the point. She was living in Phoenix at the time of the robbery. She had lost her nest egg and was working at a job that couldn't have paid very much. Yet somehow she had enough money to buy the property here, soon after the robbery, and now she lives comfortably without working at all. She's vigorous, calm, and self-reliant, which one would have to be to take part in a daring robbery. And she fits the description of the getaway driver perfectly!"

"So what!" snapped Allie. "Jupiter, you haven't got one shred of real evidence against Mrs Macomber!"

"No, I don't," admitted Jupe. "But I see a lot of strange coincidences, and we can hunt for evidence." He looked slyly at Allie. "There's still another possibility we must consider. If Mrs Macomber *was* in on the robbery of the armoured truck . . . ." Jupe paused dramatically.

"Go on, go on," Allie ordered.

"Then it's quite possible that Gilbert Morgan did not come to Twin Lakes alone. Perhaps . . . per-

D

haps he never had a chance to hide his money. . ."

"You mean Mrs Macomber shoved Morgan down that pit?" screamed Allie. "You're out of your mind, Jupiter Jones! I won't listen to another word you say!" Allie jumped up and stormed out of the barn.

Bob looked at Jupiter. "You don't really think Mrs Macomber murdered Morgan and stole his share of the loot, do you?"

"No," said Jupiter. "I simply couldn't resist suggesting it to Allie. But I wouldn't be surprised to find that Mrs Macomber did have some connection with the robbery!"

13

The Widow Disappears

AT THE END OF BREAKFAST the next day, Allie and
The Three Investigators were sitting alone in the
kitchen. Jupiter had devoured his food almost
absent-mindedly. When he finished, he stared at
his plate for a moment, then said to Allie, "What
was the name of the shop in Phoenix where Mrs
Macomber said she worked? Do you know?"

"Not that it's any of your business," replied
Allie, "but the shop was called the Teepee. Mrs
Macomber told me a lot about it. Some woman
named Mrs Harvard bought it from her and kept
her on as a saleslady. Mrs Harvard was a real miser
—Mrs Macomber once said she'd have paid her
help with Confederate money if she'd had any."

"Oh?" said Jupe. "That makes it even more
curious that Mrs Macomber was able to amass
enough to buy her property. Well, that part of her
history we can check."

"Jupiter Jones! Don't you dare go snooping into
Mrs Macomber's business!" cried Allie. "She's
okay! I like her!"

"And you *don't* like Wesley Thurgood," said
Jupe. "That doesn't mean that Wesley Thurgood
is a criminal or that Mrs Macomber is not. As a

matter of fact, I like Mrs Macomber myself. But as a detective, I can't let my personal feelings influence my judgment."

"Oh, come off it!" said Allie. "Your judgment is screwy, period. The *idea* that Mrs Macomber could be a robber!"

Jupe sighed. "Look, Allie. I don't know that Mrs Macomber has done a thing. But I do know that she was living in Phoenix when a woman remarkably like her took part in a robbery. And a hold-up man *was* found dead in a mine that she knew all about. Coincidences like that have to be investigated—they might not *be* coincidences. For a start, we can at least verify that Mrs Macomber worked all those years in that shop."

"Why don't you call Phoenix?" dared Allie. "You'll find out that she was telling the truth and you won't be any further ahead."

"That may be," conceded Jupe. Trailed by the others, he went to the telephone in the living room and got the number for the Teepee shop from Phoenix information. He dialled it and put on his deepest, most sincere, grown-up voice.

"Teepee? . . . May I speak to Mrs Harvard, if you please?"

There was a brief pause. "Mrs Harvard? said Jupe. "This is Emerson Foster of the Bon Ton Department Store in Lordsburg, New Mexico. We have an application for employment here—a Mrs Henry Macomber. She has given your name as a reference. I understand that she left the Teepee approximately five years ago. Mrs Macomber tells us that she resigned and—"

Jupe paused. The telephone made noises which the others could not understand.

"After fifteen years?" said Jupe finally.

"I told you so," whispered Allie. "She's on the level."

But Jupe was listening to the voice on the telephone, and he looked very serious. "That's . . . that's hard to believe!" he said. "Yes. Yes, well thank you for being so frank. Believe me, we appreciate it."

He hung up the telephone.

"What did she say?" asked Pete.

"Mrs Macomber worked at the Teepee for fifteen years," Jupe told them. "She left there in the spring, five years ago. Mrs Harvard said it was in April or May. She didn't remember exactly. But Mrs Macomber did not resign."

"So she was fired," said Allie. "So what?"

"She *wasn't* fired," said Jupe. "She simply didn't come to work one morning. She didn't even telephone, and when one of the women in the shop went to her apartment to see what was the matter, she was gone. She'd moved out, and left no forwarding address."

Allie looked blank.

Bob had been slouched on the sofa. Now he leaned forward. "Five years ago in the spring," he said. "That would be about the time the armoured car was held up. Jupe, you could be right. She may have driven that getaway car, and then run for it. I wonder where she was in the months between the time she left the Teepee and the time she came back to Twin Lakes."

"Lying low?" suggested Pete.

"Let's not leap to any conclusions," said Jupe. "There could be some explanation. Why don't we go across the road and see her? Perhaps we could persuade her to talk more about Phoenix and what took place that year."

"Subtle questioning," said Pete. "Jupe, you're good at that. Let's go!"

"I think you all stink!" cried Allie.

"Okay. Don't come with us," said Pete.

"Oh, I'll come all right. I want to see you fall flat on your faces when you find out you're wrong."

But when Allie and The Three Investigators crossed the road, they discovered that there would be no subtle questioning. Mrs Macomber's truck was gone and there was no answer when they knocked at her door.

"She's probably in town," said Allie. "Let's get this settled. I'll leave a note on her kitchen table and ask her to come to lunch. Magdalena won't mind."

She opened the door and went into the kitchen, followed by the boys.

"Mrs Macomber?" called Allie. When no answer came, she went on into the living room, looking for a scrap of paper. The Investigators waited in the kitchen, which was not nearly as neat as it had been the day before. There were unwashed pots on the stove, and the kitchen sink was filled with dirty dishes that looked as if they had been left overnight.

"Hey, I think Mrs Macomber is going on a trip." called Allie.

"What makes you think that?" asked Jupe, walking into the living room.

Allie pointed through the open door to Mrs Macomber's bedroom. A small suitcase lay on the bed, with some articles of clothing strewn beside it. Jupe moved forward to the bedroom door. "I think she's already left!" he said after studying the room a minute.

"Hunh?" Pete had come up behind him.

Jupe indicated the bedroom closet, which stood open. "All her clothes have been cleaned out of the closet. And look at those drawers hanging out of the bureau—they're empty. Fellows, she's gone—and I think she left quickly!"

"What do you mean?" demanded Allie.

"That all the signs indicate a very hasty departure," replied Jupe. "You saw this house yesterday. It was neat as a pin. Is Mrs Macomber the type to go away leaving bureau drawers open, extra clothes and a suitcase lying around, and dirty dishes in the sink? Never—not unless she were in a great hurry or had no choice!"

"She's been kidnapped!" cried Allie. "That guy who took her groceries yesterday . . . maybe she got a look at him and so he . . ."

"So he kidnapped her, thoughtfully packing her clothes before he took her away?" said Jupe. "That is hardly likely."

"Maybe she's away on vacation," suggested Pete.

"Doubtful," said Jupe. "She wouldn't have left the house a mess before going on vacation. And she didn't say anything yesterday about taking a holiday."

Bob said, "Maybe some family emergency came up. She might have had a call after we left."

Jupe pulled at his lower lip and frowned. "That's the best suggestion yet, Bob! But there's another possibility. She may have decided to leave because you found that Phoenix newspaper."

"But she didn't know what was in the paper," said Allie. "She said it was there when she bought this place."

"Maybe it was," conceded Jupe. "But if she took part in that robbery, and caught a glimpse of that headline yesterday, she'd know what was in the paper. And then she'd know that she was in trouble, because *you*, Allie, had to go and tell her that we were digging into the story of the dead hold-up man! She wouldn't have to think very long to realize that we might put two and two together—and might start asking her some difficult questions. And you know what she'd do then?"

"She'd run for it!" declared Pete.

"If you think that, you should put your money where your mouth is," said Allie. "Call the sheriff."

"And report what?" asked Jupiter. "That Mrs Macomber has gone away? She has every right to do that. We have no proof that she had any connection with Morgan or with the robbery. It's all conjecture."

Jupe went out and walked down the short dirt driveway to the road. He stopped, bent, and examined the tyre tracks in the dust. The others went to him, and he pointed to the most recent tracks which overlaid the traces of other vehicles. They indicated that a truck had backed out of Mrs Macomber's drive, then headed towards Wesley Thurgood's property.

"Odd," said Jupiter Jones. "She didn't drive towards town. She went the other way."

"If those marks were made by her truck," said Allie.

"They match all the tracks in her driveway," said Jupe.

Allie and The Three Investigators followed the tracks in the dusty road. Mrs Macomber's truck had been driven past Wesley Thurgood's gate. When the boys and Allie passed Thurgood's enclosure, the huge dog leaped against the fence and barked wickedly. Now that the fence was finished, the dog was no longer kept on the chain. Thurgood and his Mexican labourers were nowhere in sight.

A few hundred yards beyond Thurgood's property, they could see where the truck had turned off on to a rutted trail that was barely recognizable as a road. It went up the mountain in a series of hairpin turns.

"Why ... why she took the old Hambone Road," said Allie.

"Hambone?" questioned Jupe.

Allie pointed. "Way up there, on the top of the ridge, there's a real ghost town. It's called Hambone. There was a mine there, too, but its played out just like the Death Trap. There wasn't any sawmill to save the town, so it died. I've never been up there myself. The road is too bad. You need a four-wheel-drive jeep or truck to get up there."

"Mrs Macomber had a four-wheel-drive truck," said Jupiter, "and she certainly went that way."

Pete looked excited. "Why don't we? We can follow her trail and see what she's up to. Allie, your uncle has a four-wheel-drive truck and . . ."

"And I can only drive it on the ranch," Allie reminded him. Suddenly she brightened. "We can take the horses," she cried. "The horses could get up there. We really ought to. If Mrs Macomber had an accident on the road, or if her truck broke down she might be in bad trouble. We can pack a picnic lunch and tell Uncle Harry that we want to explore a real ghost town."

"You tell him, Allie," said Pete. "You can make up stories better than the three of us put together!"

14

The End of the Trail

MAGDALENA PREPARED a large picnic lunch for Allie and the Investigators, which they packed into saddle-bags.

"Be careful with the fire when you roast the hot dogs," Magdalena warned from the porch. "You do not wish to burn down the mountain." She waved to them as they set out.

Allie was mounted on Indian Queen, her handsome Appaloosa. Jupe, sweating slightly, was astride a stout mare. Pete sat easily on a rawboned gelding, and Bob rode the third of Uncle Harry's horses, a dappled steed. They passed Thurgood's gate at a trot, sending the dog into an outburst of barking, and drawing stares from the two Mexicans. The men were now painting Thurgood's cabin.

Allie was in the lead when they started up the mountainside. Jupe tagged close behind on the mare, who was much more interested in nibbling the grass beside the path than in getting to the top of the slope. Once Allie wheeled Queenie round and seized the reins of Jupe's horse. "You've got to hold her head up!" Allie scolded. "Come on. Get with it!"

Jupe's face went red. He tugged at the reins and

the mare quickened her pace, then she slowed and again ambled on, one plodding step after another.

"It'll take us all day to get there!" cried Allie.

"Giddap!" Jupe kicked his chubby legs against the mare's sides, but the mare kept to her stolid pace.

"No one will ever mistake you for the Lone Ranger!" said Bob. But he rode stiffly, looking down at the rugged hillside from time to time. "I'd hate to have a fall here," he muttered.

They rode on, now and then glimpsing the marks of Mrs Macomber's tyres in sandy places on the trail. Pine trees on either side blocked their view of the mountainside. It was after one when at last they reached the bare crest of the hills and found themselves ambling down the dusty main street of Hambone. All round them were tinder-dry houses with broken windows and warped, paintless boards pulling away from uprights. Rusted bedsprings lay in the street with old tin cans, battered furniture, and shards of jagged glass.

Allie dismounted and tied her Appaloosa to the railing of a porch in front of what had once been the Hambone General Store. The boys got down, moving stiffly, and secured their mounts.

"It's pretty bleak." Pete looked round as if he expected the ghost town to contain an actual ghost.

"Uncle Harry says a real ghost town gets this way," said Allie. "Vandals come in and break things and throw things out the windows." She pointed down the street to a big building very much like the one on Wesley Thurgood's property. The walls and roof were of rusted corrugated iron, and gaping holes opened on to blackness within. "That must be the mine works," Allie said.

They started towards the huge shed. "Be careful where you step," warned Allie. "And don't pick up any of those sheets of iron. The rattlesnakes like to get under things to keep out of the sun, and if you scare a rattler . . ."

"We *know* what happens if you scare a rattler!" said Pete. "Don't worry. We're not about to poke around in the junk."

They reached the doorway of the mine works and stopped. The door had long since fallen away, and Allie and the boys looked into a gloomy building.

"Wonder if that floor would hold us," said Bob. "Or is it rotten?"

"That's of no interest to us," said Jupiter. "The truck is not here. We didn't come simply to tour an abandoned town." He went to the middle of the street to examine a set of tyre tracks. "Mrs Macomber certainly reached the top of the crest," he announced. "If she hadn't, we would have found her on the trail." He went on, not stepping on the tracks, until he reached the corner of the mine works. "Aha!" he said loudly.

"What is it?" Allie darted to join him, and Pete and Bob followed her.

There, behind the ruined building, stood Mrs Macomber's truck.

"Mrs Macomber!" shouted Allie. She ran towards the truck. "Mrs Macomber! It's me! Allie!"

She had almost reached the truck when there was a nasty whirring sound.

"Allie! Stand still!" shouted Jupe.

Allie tried to throw herself backwards. Her feet slipped from under her and she went down. A deadly, sinister shape seemed to fly from beneath the truck. Allie flung herself to one side, and a wicked head with fearful wide jaws and lethal fangs struck at the spot where, an instant before, she had been.

Allie didn't move.

The rattler lay stretched to its full length for just a second, then once more sounded its hideous warning and began to pull its body into coils.

"Keep still!" whispered Pete. He picked up a large stone, took careful aim, and hurled it at the rattler.

"Bull's-eye!" cried Bob. "Right on the head! Boy that was close."

Allie scrambled to her feet and looked with horror at the struggling, writhing snake. "Thanks," was all she said to Pete, but she was very pale and shaking.

"Nothing any well-trained boy scout wouldn't do," said Pete. He crouched and peered under the truck, making sure he kept a safe distance. "Guess that was the only rattler there," he said.

Allie and the boys stepped round the dying snake and began to examine Mrs Macomber's truck. It was empty. There was no luggage of any kind, and there were no keys in the ignition.

"If she was called away on a family emergency, she wouldn't have left the truck here," said Bob.

"I don't get it," said Allie. "Where'd she go, and where is her stuff?"

"Could she be hiding someplace?" wondered Pete.

They searched the town, peering through windows, opening doors that moved on rusty hinges. They found nothing but broken furniture and heaped-up rubbish. Here and there they found footprints. But they saw no trace of Mrs Macomber.

"There *have* been people here," said Jupe. "A number of people." They returned to the truck and stared at the ground. There were footprints—some been made by Allie and the boys, but some had not. Twenty yards from the truck there were the marks of a second set of tyres.

"Someone else came here in a jeep or a truck," said Pete. They followed the tyre tracks along the street to the edge of the abandoned town. There, leading down the far side of the mountain, was a road—a narrow road, but one that was still in fair condition.

Jupiter was quiet for a moment. "She could have arranged to meet someone here," he said. "Yes . . . that's it. She drove up from Twin Lakes, transferred her belongings to another vehicle, abandoned her truck, and left. Allie, where does this road go?"

"I'm not sure," Allie admitted. "I've never been here before. But I know there's a lot of desert on the other side of the mountains."

A cloud of dust billowed above the trees on the slope below them, and they heard the sound of a motor labouring up the grade.

"She's coming back!" exclaimed Pete.

But it was not Mrs Macomber returning. Instead, a jeep appeared, bouncing slightly and skidding on loose gravel. At the wheel was an elderly man who wore a wide-brimmed straw hat. A woman in a printed cotton dress sat beside him.

"Hi there!" The man grinned and stopped his jeep.

"Hi!" said Pete.

"You youngsters here by yourselves?" the man asked.

Pete nodded.

"Bottle hunting, I suppose?" said the man.

"Bottle hunting?" asked Bob.

"That's what we come for," the woman told them. "We drove all the way from Casa Verde to these old towns in the hills. If you're lucky you can find some wonderful old bottles in these places. Got to watch it, though. Don't touch anything with your hands. If you want to move something, use a stick. Snakes around here."

"We know," said Jupiter. "Have . . . are there lots of people who drive up here?"

"I suppose," said the man. "The road up here to Hambone wasn't bad. Even if you don't find any bottles, these old places are interesting. I found a kerosene lantern in one ghost town last week. It was good as new."

He drove the jeep on and parked near the store.

"So much for the other tyre tracks," said Bob. "Those could have been made by someone who came to meet Mrs Macomber or they could have belonged to any antique hunter."

Jupiter sighed. "It doesn't really matter, does it? Mrs Macomber was here, but she isn't here now. We've reached the end of the trail."

15

The Silent Watchdog

AFTER ROASTING THEIR HOT DOGS, Allie and the Investigators got back on their mounts. The return journey to Twin Lakes was slow, with the horses sticking close together and picking their way cautiously down the steep slope from Hambone.

"I wouldn't have believed it," said Jupe. "Mrs. Macomber appeared to be a self-possessed woman, yet she seems to have panicked and run."

"You're just guessing," Allie told him. "We don't know everything that happens with Mrs Macomber. There might be another explanation."

"There seems to be only one," said Jupiter. "When she realized that we had been investigating what went on here five years ago, she got frightened and fled. Perhaps one of her confederates met her in Hambone. It is even possible that another member of the hold-up gang has been lurking around Twin Lakes for the last few days. We still do not have any explanation for the prowler who took the machete from the barn."

Pete brightened. "Hey! He could have been part of the hold-up gang. Mrs Macomber could have hidden him when the sheriff searched for him that night."

"And what about the groceries . . . and the cigarette butt?" added Bob.

"What about them?" Allie asked.

"Just listen for a minute," said Bob. "Suppose Mrs Macomber was hiding the prowler—let's just say he was part of the gang. He could have been somewhere nearby when we went to see her yesterday. He might have gotten hungry and decided to grab a snack while we were going through her houses. Remember, it wasn't Mrs Macomber who first missed the food. It was Jupe who noticed that the things were gone."

"Good thinking, Bob," said Jupe.

"You're all nuts!" said Allie.

"Don't get upset, Allie," said Jupe. "Remember, we *are* only guessing. At this point we have a number of odd things going on. We have found the five-year-old corpse of a man who may or may not have been involved in a hold-up five years ago. We also have a widow who just might have been involved—and who has mysteriously disappeared. We have a prowler who stole a machete and who may or may not have been a confederate of the widow, or of the dead man in the mine. We also have the mine—a played-out silver mine that is seemingly being worked by a wealthy real estate man from Los Angeles. And we have a gold pebble from that mine. According to Mrs Macomber, the mine never contained an ounce of gold."

"Mrs Macomber might have lied," said Pete.

"Whatever her connection with the dead man, there would be no reason for her to lie about the gold," Jupe pointed out. "She seems to have no connection whatsoever with Wesley Thurgood, except that she remembers his birth here in Twin Lakes."

"Don't forget the loot from the robbery," Pete said. "If it was ever here, did Thurgood get it? Or did Mrs Macomber get it five years ago?"

The four were silent for the rest of the trip down the mountain. By the time they reached the bottom it was late afternoon. As Thurgood's compound came into view, they saw that his red passenger truck was gone. There were buckets of paint near Thurgood's cabin, but the job had not been finished, and the Mexican labourers were nowhere to be seen. The huge watchdog was stretched out, sleeping in the sun.

The horses clip-clopped past Thurgood's closed, padlocked gate. The dog slept on.

"That's strange," said Jupe. "He's usually trying to tear the fence down to get at us."

When they reached Harrison Osborne's pasture they unsaddled the horses. The front door of the house was open and there was a note on the kitchen table: "Magdalena's sister needs her. I am driving her to Silver City and we'll be back late tonight. Take cold cuts for dinner and *keep out of trouble!* Love, Uncle Harry."

"How nice!" Jupiter's solemn face brightened.

"I don't think it's nice—what if Magdalena's sister is sick? What's the matter with you, Jupiter Jones?" asked Allie.

"Let us hope that Magdalena's sister is not ill," said Jupe. "What's nice is that no one is here. Mrs Macomber is gone. Thurgood's truck is missing,

116

and his two labourers are not about. Your uncle and Magdalena are away. The coast is clear—and we're free to investigate the one mysterious event that we haven't yet looked into: the appearance of a bit of gold in a played-out silver mine."

Jupe took the pebble from his pocket, tossed it into the air, then looked eagerly at his companions. "Let's go—while we have a chance! We've got to find out what's happening in that mine."

"You forgot the watchdog," said Pete. "The dog is there, and he isn't chained up, either."

"Don't worry about the dog!" Allie flew to the refrigerator, and yanked out the remains of the leg of lamb they had had for dinner the night before. "Plenty of meat on this, and a nice bone to chew. It should keep old Fido busy for a spell."

A few minutes later The Three Investigators and Allie were hurrying across the Christmas-tree field towards the mine. When they reached the edge of Uncle Harry's land, they looked through the fence into Thurgood's enclosure. The dog still slept.

"Hey!" Pete shouted. "Hey, Rex! Rover! Yahoo, Rover!"

"Come and get it, pooch!" Allie brandished the leg of lamb.

The dog did not stir.

Pete called to the dog once more. When he did not move, the tall investigator took hold of the fence, scrambled to the top, and jumped down into Thurgood's clearing.

"Watch it," warned Bob.

"Toss the bone over," said Pete. "If the dog

wakes up, I'll throw it to him."

Allie threw the bone to Pete. He stood watching the dog. "You'd almost think he was dead," he said.

"Let's just take advantage of the situation," said Allie. And she, too, climbed to the top of the eight-foot fence and then down to the ground. Bob followed her example, and Jupe—with some huffing and puffing—managed to push his bulk over.

The four warily approached the dog. Allie kept talking to the animal. "There, boy. Easy there!" she crooned.

"Careful!" whispered Jupiter.

She leaned over and touched the dog. He twitched and whimpered as if he were dreaming.

"Well, he's only sleeping," said Allie. "But how come he doesn't wake up?"

Jupe spied a tin pan near the fence. He picked it up and sniffed at a few scraps of raw meat that remained on it. "I can't smell anything, but the dog may have been drugged," he announced. "Perhaps someone wanted him out of the way!"

The others looked around apprehensively, but no other person could be seen.

"I wonder where the Mexican men are—the ones who work for Thurgood." Without realizing it, Bob had lowered his voice to a whisper.

"Hello!" shouted Pete. "Is anybody here?"

The cry echoed and re-echoed from the hillside.

"Pipe down!" snapped Allie. "So somebody drugged the dog and no one's here." She pulled out the flashlight she had stuck in her back pocket. "Let's move fast before somebody does show up."

She started towards the mine entrance, which lay in deep shadow now that the sun had disappeared behind the mountain. It would be dusk soon.

Just inside the mine were several shovels and a wheelbarrow. Allie flashed her light on the tunnel walls and up over the timbers that supported the ceiling. "What have they been doing here?" she said. "I don't see where anybody's been blasting."

"We haven't gone in far enough yet," said Jupe. "The sound of those explosions were muffled. Let's go on to the place where I found the pebble."

He took the light and led the way to the spot where the tunnel branched out to the right and the left. He turned left without hesitation. "It was about fifty feet from here," he said, and he paced forward.

Now there was a bigger pile of loose rock and pebbles on the floor of the mine. Above the heap of rubble was a wide hole that had been blasted in one wall. Something glittered at the edge of the cavity.

"Look!" cried Pete. "Gold!"

Jupe stepped forward and held the light close to the tunnel wall. Bright specks glinted under the torch's beam. "Amazing!" said Jupe. With his finger-nails he dug a bit of shining yellow metal out of the hard earth. He turned the light full on his prize and stared at it.

"So Mrs Macomber was wrong!" said Allie. "There *is* gold in the mine!"

Suddenly all four of them froze.

Very faintly, from somewhere outside the mine, came the sound of what could have been a shot, or perhaps a car backfiring.

"Someone's coming!" whispered Pete.

"We'd better scram!" said Allie. "I don't want to get caught in here again!"

Jupe put the bit of gold into his pocket and they hurried towards the main tunnel. The timbered entrance now showed only as a faint square of light. When they glimpsed it, Jupe snapped off the flashlight and they groped towards the fresh air, stumbling up the slanting floor of the tunnel. At the mine entrance, Jupe stopped them.

The dog still lay in the clearing, almost invisible in the gathering dusk. A car screeched to a halt outside the fence. Allie and the boys watched two men get out of the car.

"Okay, Gasper," said one of the men. "Grab a rock or something and we'll get that padlock off the gate."

"No sweat, Manny," said the second, in a rasping wheeze. "I'll shoot it off!"

"You crazy?" said the first man. "Somebody hears you and that fat-cat sheriff will be up here. Get a rock."

Even from where they stood, yards from the gate, Allie and the boys could hear the laboured breathing of the man called Gasper.

"Jupe!" Pete whispered. "That sound. It's the prowler who was in the barn! The one who took a whack at me with the machete! He breathed like that!"

They shrank back into the darkness of the mine tunnel.

"What are we going to do?" whispered Allie. "If we try to make a run for it, those creeps are sure to see us—and I don't think they're here on a friendly visit! There's not a soul up here tonight—*or* back at the ranch!"

They could hear the man called Gasper pounding at the padlock on Thurgood's gate. The lock dropped to the ground and the gate was pushed open.

"If it's still here, it's probably in the house," croaked Gasper.

The two men crossed the clearing to Thurgood's cabin. "Might not be here at all," said his partner. "He's had plenty of time to stash it someplace else."

"If we don't find it here, we can check out the mine," said Gasper.

"And if we don't find it there," Manny replied, "we wait for that crumb to come back and we *force* him to tell us what he did with it!"

The two men laughed as they went into Thurgood's cabin.

Allie almost squealed. "They're going to catch us in here," she cried. "We've got to try and make it to the ranch. We can call the sheriff from there."

"Are you crazy, Allie?" whispered Pete. "Those guys are armed!"

"But she's right," said Bob. "We've got to do something!"

Jupe crawled to the entrance of the mine and looked out. A bucket of liquid stood nearby, next to the rickety shack that Thurgood had padlocked some days before. Jupe crept forward and sniffed the bucket, then looked at the tinder-dry wood of the shack.

He slipped back to the entrance of the tunnel. "The Mexicans left a bucket of paint thinner next to Thurgood's shack," he reported. "If we set fire to the shack someone in town is sure to see it and alert the fire department. We'll get the fire truck and probably the sheriff up here in no time—and those thugs will be trapped. Pete, you took matches to Hambone today. Do you still have them?"

Pete took a book of matches out of his pocket and he and Jupe crept outside. Jupe picked up the bucket and sloshed its contents over the shack. Pete struck a match and tossed it. Instantly a sheet of flame engulfed the old wood. The shed was burning fiercely.

"Beautiful!" said Pete. "That ought to do it."

Suddenly Jupe gasped and shouted: "It sure will! Quick! Get into the mine. I think I know what Thurgood was storing in that shack!"

They dodged into the mine entrance and the four scrambled down the slanting floor.

"Get down!" yelled Jupe.

They all hit the ground—and the shack exploded with a roar that shook the earth!

16

Flight!

THE EXPLOSION WENT ON AND ON, thunderous and deafening. When at last it stopped, echoes of the blast rumbled back from the hills. Allie and the boys stumbled out of the mine. The remains of the shed blazed beside the mine entrance, and bits of burning debris were strewn over the ground.

Pete gaped. "All we wanted was a little fire!"

"I should have guessed that Thurgood was keeping his dynamite in that shack!" said Jupiter.

As the shock of the explosion wore off, things started happening with frightening speed. The door of the old mine works building sprang open and the two Mexicans rushed out. They scrambled over the fence and disappeared among the rocks on the slope above the mine. Manny and Gasper staggered out of the cabin just as Thurgood's red truck careered into the clearing through the open gate.

"Hey, Mr Thurgood!" yelled Pete as he ran forward. "Watch out! Those guys broke into your house, and they're armed!"

As Gasper turned threateningly to Pete, Thurgood jumped out of his truck, pulling a shotgun after him. "Hold it right there," he yelled. "If you take another step, you're finished."

But Gasper was too fast for him. Before Thurgood could raise his gun barrel, the thug lunged at Pete and grabbed the boy's shoulder. Pete stumbled and felt something press into the small of his back.

"Drop your gun," Gasper told Thurgood, "or I'll blow the kid in half!"

Thurgood lowered his gun slowly, then let it fall to the ground. Manny ran forward and picked it up. A nasty grin spread over his flat features. His eyes darted to the other kids near the mouth of the mine. "You girl!" he called. "Get over here!"

"No, wait!" Bob tried to step in front of Allie.

"Out of the way, kid!" ordered Manny. Brandishing the shotgun, he ran over and grabbed Allie, twisting her arm behind her back. "Now march!"

Suddenly they heard the wail of a siren. It was the fire engine coming from Twin Lakes.

Manny and Gasper looked at each other, and tightened their hold on the hostages.

"That road..." Manny nodded towards the rutted track up to Hambone, faintly visible in the failing light. "Where's it go, girlie?"

"Just... just to an old ghost town," said Allie.

"What's on the other side of them mountains?"

"Only the desert." Allie looked frightened, but she held her chin high.

Gasper nodded towards Thurgood's truck. "We can make it in that. It's got four-wheel drive."

"You'll never get away with this!" cried Allie.

"Shut up!" croaked Gasper.

They could hear the distant rumble of the fire engine now. Again the siren sounded.

"Hurry up! Into the truck!" Manny shoved Allie in front of him, thrust her into the back seat of Thurgood's truck, and climbed in after her. Pete ended up in the front seat next to Gasper. Jupe, Bob and Thurgood stood by helplessly. The truck lurched out of the clearing and, with a clash of gears, started up the slope of the Hambone road.

Jupe and Bob ran to the gate after the departing truck. Gasper was driving without lights, and the truck was soon lost from sight among the pine trees on the mountainside. In the other direction, the red lights of the approaching fire engine showed beyond Uncle Harry's gate. Siren screaming, it pulled into Thurgood's clearing a few minutes later. The sheriff's car raced in after it and braked abruptly.

Sheriff Tait got out and glanced at the wreck of the shack, which was now a glowing heap. "Looks like the emergency's over, Sam," said the sheriff to the man at the wheel of the fire engine. Then Tait came towards Wesley Thurgood. "What happened?" he demanded. "Sounded in town like the whole mountain fell on you."

Jupiter stepped forward quickly. "I set fire to the shack," he said. "There were two men breaking into Mr Thurgood's cabin and I wanted to attract some attention—but that's not important now! Those men have Allie Jamison and Peter Crenshaw with them! They took Mr Thurgood's truck up the Hambone road. They're armed . . .

and they seem desperate men to me!"

Sheriff Tait stared off into the darkness that now shrouded the mountains. "Somebody took Allie?"

"And our friend Pete Crenshaw," insisted Jupiter. "At gunpoint!"

The sheriff rubbed a big hand across his chin. He scowled. "How long have they been gone?"

"Just a few minutes. You can catch up with them if you hurry. They're driving without lights, so they can't be going very fast."

"They'll go fast enough if they see me behind them. Might well run off the road. Chasing them is mighty risky when they've got those kids along."

"Then wait for them on the other side of the mountain," urged Jupe. "When they reach Hambone, they'll certainly keep going. If the road is blocked on the far side of the ridge . . ."

"Which road?" said the sheriff.

Jupiter gaped. "There's more than one road?"

"Son, if they make it to Hambone. They've got a dozen different routes they can take. There's lots of little dirt roads on the other side of the hills. They branch off from the main Hambone road and run to little cabins and some old mines. Then they meander on down to the desert. Those guys can stay hidden in the hills for weeks if they want to."

"But they can't," shouted Bob. "They've got Allie and Pete!"

The sheriff went to his car and reached in to take the speaker from his two-way radio. "I can have a helicopter from the highway patrol here in less than half an hour," he said. "And I'll tell them to cover the foothills on the far side by car. Let's just pray those bandits don't decide they can move faster if they get rid of a couple of hostages!"

17

Breakdown

JIM HOOVER, THE HELICOPTER PILOT, grinned and nodded when Jupe and Bob begged to go along on the search for the fleeing thugs.

"I don't like it," Sheriff Tait complained. "It could be dangerous." But he stood aside so the boys could squeeze into the helicopter and kneel behind the seats for pilot and passenger. The sheriff climbed into the passenger seat and laid a rifle with a telescopic sight across his knees.

"All set?" said Hoover. He lifted the chopper off the road near Thurgood's mine. Except for the pale light of a crescent moon, it was now pitch dark. As soon as they were airborne Hoover flipped a switch. The blue-white beam of a searchlight stabbed the night. "You can control the light from there," said Hoover to Sheriff Tait. He indicated a lever in front of the sheriff's seat.

Sheriff Tait leaned forward. "They must still be running without lights." The sheriff manipulated the handle and the searchlight swept across the slope below. They could see rocks and huge boulders that cast grotesque shadows. They could see parts of the narrow, twisting ribbon of road that led from Twin Lakes to Hambone. It appeared almost white among the dark evergreen trees that crowded close to it on either side.

"Unless they ditch the truck, they've got to stick to that road at least as far as Hambone," said Hoover.

The helicopter veered towards the mountain and Jupe felt his stomach lurch. He gasped.

"Take it easy, kid," said Hoover. "Make believe you're riding in an elevator that goes sideways instead of just up and down."

"I'm fine!" declared Jupe. "Perfectly fine!"

The helicopter covered every inch of the road between Twin Lakes and Hambone. There was no truck.

"Man, they were making time to get over the ridge this fast," said the sheriff as they skimmed above the crest of the mountain. "And without lights!"

Bob wondered. Had Manny and Gasper really managed to get to the top of the rise and beyond? Or had Gasper run the truck off the road in the darkness? Were Pete and Allie all right? Or were they lying below, caught in the wreckage of the truck, possibly hurt?

Bob hunched his shoulders. Sheriff Tait must have sensed his fear. "Don't worry, son," he said kindly "My deputy and another guy will come up the road in a jeep. If anything happened to that truck, they'll find it."

Jim Hoover took his craft low over the roofs of Hambone, and the searchlight probed the open areas between the rotting old buildings.

"What's that?" cried the sheriff. "There's a

E

truck down there . . . behind the old Hambone mine works!"

Jupiter leaned forward. "That's Mrs Macomber's pick-up," he said. "We found it abandoned there this afternoon. And we don't know *where* Mrs Macomber is."

"What is going on around here?" demanded Sheriff Tait.

"I think I can explain it all later," said Jupe. "Right now we've got to find Allie and Pete."

"Well, if they got past Hambone they're somewhere on the west slope, down on one of those little roads," said the sheriff. "But I'm blessed if I know which one I'd take if I were on the lam with a couple of kids."

"There's only one way to find out," said Jim Hoover. The helicopter clattered on towards the west, leaving Hambone to its echoes and its ghosts.

Allie and Pete sat in the truck with Manny and Gasper and listened to the helicopter as it hovered above them. The searchlight on the craft swept the treetops and touched the empty road that led up to the ruined town. For an instant it touched the evergreen trees under which Gasper had driven the truck.

Allie Jamison held her breath. With all her might she willed the searchers in the helicopter to spot them. "Please see us!" she pleaded in her mind. "Please! We're right down here! Can't you see us?"

The sound of the helicopter grew fainter, then faded away. Gasper chuckled. "C'mon. Let's move. He put the truck into gear, and it roared and shuddered as it lumbered out of the gully by the side of the road. Then, still without lights, they started slowly up to Hambone again.

"If we get away clean, I'm never coming back." Gasper's voice was morose. "Wouldn't get us anything, anyway. If that Thurgood creep hasn't found the stuff yet, he'll sure start looking now. Don't take no genius to figure out we were after something big."

"How big *was* Gilbert Morgan's share of that quarter of a million dollars?" said Allie.

Gasper stamped on the brake and the truck screeched to a stop. "Who said anything about a quarter of a million dollars?" he demanded. When Allie didn't answer he fumbled a cigarette out of his pocket and lit it. "We ought to dump these two some place," he told Manny. "Some place where nobody will ever find them."

Allie coughed loudly and waved cigarette smoke away from her face. "A terrible habit, smoking," she said. "Ruins your wind—in case you haven't noticed—and it does horrible things to your voice. And it wouldn't do you any good to get rid of us. We know about the robbery in Phoenix five years ago. There were four crooks—three men and a woman. Gilbert Morgan was one of the men, wasn't he? And you're the other two. We know, and so do Bob and Jupe."

Manny groaned. "The other two kids. And we left them behind!"

"Stupid of you, wasn't it?" said Allie.

Manny held up the shotgun, and Allie was silent.

Soon they reached Hambone and started down the other side of the mountain. Gasper let the truck roll, holding it in check with the low gear. After a time they came to a place where the main road curved off to the right, and a narrower, rougher way opened to the left. Gasper crushed a cigarette stub in the already overflowing ashtray and pointed to the main road. "Where's that go?" he asked Allie.

"I don't know," said Allie, waving smoke away from her face. "Down to the desert, I suppose."

"Take the side road," ordered Manny. "I've got a hunch that by this time there are about a hundred cops waiting for us at the bottom of the main road."

Gasper grunted and turned the truck on to the narrower road. It was barely more than a pair of tyre tracks winding among the trees. The truck lurched and rocked, but Gasper fought the wheel and kept going. The thug tossed a newly lit cigarette out the window and held on to the wheel with both hands.

"If you set the mountain on fire the whole highway patrol will find us in a minute!" said Allie snidely. Gasper was too busy controlling the truck to reply.

It seemed to Pete and Allie that they travelled through the hills for eternities. Sometimes they saw cabins, dark and secret, nestled under the trees. Once they came upon a settlement that was smaller than Hambone and even more ruined. A coyote loped away, keeping to the shadows. Several times they again saw the searchlight of an approaching helicopter, and Gasper pulled off the road and waited until it disappeared. Pete and Allie tried to doze, but the lurching of the truck kept waking them up.

For a while they seemed to be climbing higher and higher. But at last the road became a series of switchbacks that zigzagged down the slope. "I think we've got it made." Gasper's hands were tight on the wheel. The moon had set and only the faint light from the stars that powdered the sky showed the way. The rutted track widened and levelled off, and they were at the foot of the hills. A paved highway ran across their path in front of them. On the other side of the highway was the open emptiness of the desert.

Gasper stopped the truck and looked cautiously to the left and the right. Manny chuckled. "No cops," he said. "Like I figured, they're all back at the main drag waiting for us."

"They could be anyplace." Gasper took a deep rasping breath and coughed. "We don't want that road," he decided, nodding towards the paved highway. He put the truck into first and it rolled out from beneath the trees, crossed the highway, and bounced on to the desert floor.

"Ouch!" cried Allie as the truck hit a chuckhole and she was thrown forward. "This truck will never make it!"

"Shut up!" snarled Gasper, nervously crushing out the cigarette he had just lit. "We're bound to pick up another road if we keep going straight ahead long enough—and we need one the cops aren't watching."

The last stars faded. Pete looked back to see a faint glow behind the mountains. When at last the sun came up above the hills, the highway was far behind them and out of sight.

"There's got to be another road soon," muttered Gasper. "One that doesn't connect—"

He broke off as the truck hit a large chuckhole and they were all jerked violently to one side. There was a loud hissing sound, and steam and fumes from the fluid in the radiator filled their nostrils.

"Blast!" Gasper killed the engine, jumped out, and ran to the front of the truck. He stood and glared at the wheels as a puddle of rusty-coloured water darkened the white dust beneath the truck.

"What is it?" demanded Manny.

"The radiator's busted," said Gasper. "And the axle broke!"

Manny groaned. "You stupid idiot!"

Gasper came to the side of the truck and pointed his gun at Allie and Pete. "Okay, out! We'll hike for it!"

"You're crazy!" cried Allie.

"Shut up and move!" snarled Gasper.

Allie and Pete got out. So did Manny, who stood and looked across the flat wasteland. "That way," he decided, pointing ahead. "We'll walk that way and keep the mountains behind us. Sooner or later we'll come to something."

"No!" said Allie. "You can walk for miles and

miles out here and not come to anything. And once the sun is really up, it'll be over a hundred degrees out in the open desert—way over a hundred. We've got to stay with the truck."

"If we stay with the truck, we're dead," said Manny.

"We're dead if we leave it," Allie insisted.

"Knock that off and move!" shouted Gasper.

"No." Allie sat down on the ground. "You can shoot me if you want to, but I'm staying here. I'd rather be shot than die of the heat, or go off my rocker from thirst!" She glared at Manny and Gasper defiantly.

Pete hesitated. Then he, too, sat down beside the truck.

Gasper gave them a menacing look. His fingers tightened on the handle of his gun. Then Manny abruptly turned and stomped off across the desert.

Gasper looked from Pete and Allie to the determined figure of his crony. Then he followed Manny.

Allie and Pete watched until the two gunmen were tiny wavering shapes in the distance. The sun was climbing fast, and heat waves were beginning to shimmer on the desert floor.

"Suppose they've stopped looking for us?" Pete said. His voice was hoarse with anxiety. "We could die of thirst right here!"

18

Stranded in the Desert

HIGH IN THE AIR, Bob and Jupiter watched the mountains turn pink in the dawn light. Sheriff Tait clicked off the helicopter's searchlight and yawned. After a night of searching the hills, their eyes were red-rimmed and sore. Jim Hoover, the pilot, shifted his weight and made still another turn over the mountains.

"I don't know how they got over the ridge and off the mountain without us spotting them," said Sheriff Tait. "But I'll be darned if they're still in these hills. We've combed every inch of them."

"But where else could they be?" asked Bob. "If they'd come down on the main road the patrol cars would have caught them. And that other 'copter pilot radioed that he'd checked out the highway."

"Maybe they *will* stay in the hills," said Jupe. "There are all kinds of abandoned towns down there, and plenty of trees to hide the truck under."

"You could be right, Jupiter," said the sheriff. "But my bet is they've come down on one of the unused roads and set out across the desert. After all, they don't have any supplies, and they can't go too long without food."

"Could we find them if they're in the desert?" asked Bob.

"Sure, if we look long enough," the sheriff replied. "The desert's big, but at least it's open. Let's try there."

Jim Hoover nodded and turned west. The helicopter left the hills and flew out over the desert.

Allie fished a bandanna out of her jeans pocket and mopped her forehead. The sun beat down with white-hot intensity. She was dead tired, but too anxious to sleep. She walked around the truck for the fifth time that morning, then plopped down next to Pete, who sat in the vanishing shade of the truck. "It's getting late," she said. "It must be close to noon. Why haven't they found us yet?"

Pete nodded glumly. "And we haven't eaten since yesterday's picnic in Hambone. I'm starved."

"How can you think about food?" snapped Allie. "My mouth's so dry it feels like a cactus!"

"If the radiator hadn't cracked we could drink what was in there," said Pete.

"Ugh!" said Allie, and she hunched her shoulders. Then suddenly she shouted, "Oh my gosh! What's the matter with me?"

"What do you mean?" said Pete, startled.

Allie jumped to her feet and took the keys from the truck's ignition. She opened the large glove compartment, rummaged around, and pulled out a first-aid kit. Inside it she found a pair of surgical scissors.

"What are you going to do with those?" asked Pete as Allie waved the scissors triumphantly.

She pointed to a barrel cactus nearby. "We can cut a couple of chunks out of that cactus over there," she said. "There's *always* water stored in cactus. They sop it up when it rains and hold it so they can live through the dry spells. I don't know why I didn't think of it before!"

"Better late than never!" said Pete. "Boy, I could sure use a taste of something wet." He took the scissors and ran over to the cactus. He whacked at the tough-skinned plant until he had cut out two chunks of moist pulp. Then he handed one to Allie and bit into the other. They both screwed up their faces.

"I don't know what's worse," said Pete. "Dying of thirst . . . or this!"

Allie slowly chewed all the moisture from the cactus, then she spit out the pulp. Now the sun was almost directly overhead. "We can take cover under the truck," said Allie. "If the helicopter is still looking, they'll be able to spot it."

The two crawled into the shade beneath the truck. "It really is cooler under here," said Pete, as he stretched out and prepared to wait.

Feeling somewhat better, Allie and Pete grew more alert. They heard the faint call of a desert bird, and saw a kangaroo rat stick its head out of the ground, then scurry back out of sight. Several lizards crawled by the truck in search of food. All around, the flat expanse of wasteland shimmered in the hot sun. After what seemed like hours Pete lifted his head. Then Allie perked up. "I heard it too!" she said. Far away, they could hear the unmistakable clatter of a helicopter.

"They're coming!" Allie cried. She and Pete scrambled out from beneath the truck and ran out into the open. But the faint chattering noise died away. They searched the sky, but they could see nothing but blue. "I *know* I heard a helicopter," said Allie.

They both listened again, but they no longer heard a sound.

"Oh, why don't they come?" Allie cried. "We're as good as dead if they don't get here soon."

"Stop that, Allie," said Pete. "They'll find us— I'm sure of it." But his voice didn't sound as hopeful as his words.

Then they heard the sound again. A chopper was flying in the distance. Pete and Allie jumped up and down, waving their arms and yelling wildly. "We're here!" screamed Allie. "Down here."

Now the helicopter had spotted them. It swerved and flew in their direction. As it settled slowly to the ground, Pete and Allie ran forward, bending to avoid the whirling blades.

Sheriff Tait scrambled out of the chopper. "Are you kids all right?" he demanded.

"We're fine," said Allie. "Really!"

Pete pointed across the desert. "The crooks went that way—on foot!" he said.

"They decided to hike for it after they wrecked the truck," Allie added.

The sheriff laughed. "Reckon they're sorry now."

Jupiter and Bob were bursting to get out of the helicopter and grab their friends. But the sheriff climbed quickly back into the front seat and said something to Jim Hoover. The pilot nodded and spoke into his radio. Then he leaned out of his window and shouted to Pete and Allie above the roar of the chopper's engine, "We don't have enough room to get you two in here. But I've called for one of the other helicopters. It'll be here in five minutes. We're going after your kidnappers!" With that, he handed a canteen out to Pete, lifted the helicopter up, and headed west in search of Manny and Gasper.

Pete and Allie grinned at each other.

"I'll bet those creeps didn't get very far," said Allie with satisfaction.

19

The Millionaire's Secret

ALLIE WAS RIGHT. An hour later Manny and Gasper were brought into Twin Lakes and deposited in the clearing near Wesley Thurgood's cabin by a helicopter pilot and a deputy. The disgruntled crooks were sunburned, blistered, and exhausted. They had managed to walk only a few miles through the desert before collapsing from the heat. Allie and Pete, who had been airlifted back to Twin Lakes earlier, smiled with glee as the hand-cuffed thugs were led out of the helicopter.

A moment later, Sheriff Tait arrived with Jupe and Bob. The boys jubilantly greeted their friends, and said hello to a relieved Uncle Harry. Magdalena was there, busily passing sandwiches round and fussing over the two Mexican labourers. They had returned to the mine compound during the night and now sat on the steps of Thurgood's cabin, subdued and frightened and refusing to speak to anyone. Thurgood's dog lay chained beside the cabin, panting quietly. Thurgood himself stood nearby, looking strained and bewildered.

"Now that everyone is back," he said, "would someone please tell me who those men are—" he nodded to the manacled crooks "—and what's been going on here?"

Ignoring Thurgood, Allie turned to Jupe and exclaimed, "We guessed right about Gilbert Morgan! He was in on that armoured car hold-up in Phoenix five years ago—and those two guys were in it with him! They admitted it last night, when we were driving over the mountain."

"We didn't say a thing," declared Manny.

"Yes, you did," said Allie. "When I told you that we knew about the robbery, you said you ought to dump us. Knock us off, I guess. That's just the same as admitting it!"

Jupiter Jones smiled like a contented cherub. "So we *were* correct in our reconstruction," he said. "Everything's beginning to fall into place."

"What *are* you talking about?" demanded Sheriff Tait.

"Maybe you'd like to clue us in, Jupiter," said Uncle Harry. "I'm as much in the dark as anyone."

"I can try," said Jupe with obvious relish. He wolfed down the last of a sandwich and took a deep breath.

"When the dead man in the mine was identified as a wanted parole-jumper—a convicted hold-up artist—we wondered what such a person had been doing in such a remote place as Twin Lakes. What had drawn him to Death Trap Mine? So we checked the back issues of the *Twin Lakes Gazette* and found that several interesting events took place here five years ago.

"We knew that five years ago Gilbert Morgan's body was sealed in the mine. On the same day that the mine was sealed, a car stolen from Lordsburg was found near the mine. We could only guess that Morgan came here in that car. So we tried to trace Morgan to Lordsburg, but all we found there was an announcement in the Lordsburg newspaper of the sealing of the Death Trap Mine.

"Five years ago Mrs Macomber returned to Twin Lakes and purchased her property. In one of her abandoned houses we found a five-year-old Phoenix newspaper that contained the story of a robbery there—a robbery that netted three men and a woman at least a quarter of a million dollars. That newspaper was dated just days before the sealing of the mine—which was several months before Mrs Macomber took possession of her property. It seemed quite possible that Gilbert Morgan brought the paper here—that he was in the house before he entered the mine. We guessed that Morgan was one of the hold-up men. We now know that he was—and that you are the other two." Jupiter smiled at Manny and Gasper.

"When that body was found in the mine last week, this place was overrun with curiosity seekers. You, Gasper, came here at the same time—when you heard the news of the discovery of Morgan's corpse. You got into Harrison Osborne's barn, and when we surprised you, you attacked Pete with a machete. But you were looking for something. You had to stay on. So you hung round here, perhaps on Mrs Macomber's place. I'm sure you were the one who stole food from her kitchen and left a cigarette butt in her sink. Or did she give you food willingly?"

Gasper didn't answer.

"No matter," said Jupe. "Manny must have been round somewhere, too, but we never saw a trace of him. I guess you, Gasper, were the lookout. Yesterday afternoon the coast was clear. Everyone in the neighbourhood seemed to be away. So you drugged Thurgood's dog with some doctored meat, went and got Manny, and came to look for Morgan's share of the robbery loot."

Jupe turned to Wesley Thurgood. "You did find that money in the mine, didn't you, Mr Thurgood?"

Thurgood shook his head. "Sorry, kid, but you're on the wrong track. I admit I didn't examine the mine completely when I first opened it. But the sheriff went through it after the hood's body was found. There is nothing in that mine."

"Nothing, Mr Thurgood?" said Jupiter. He took a pebble out of his pocket and tossed it into the air. "Not even . . . not even gold?"

Thurgood looked startled.

"Gold?" said Sheriff Tait. "There was never any gold in the old Death Trap."

"There is gold now," said Jupiter. "I picked this pebble up in the mine the day Allie found Morgan's body. I showed it to a jeweller in Lordsburg. He said that the bit of shiny reddish metal in it is gold—gold with a high percentage of copper."

The sheriff looked stunned. "But . . . but if there is gold in the Death Trap Mine why didn't anyone find it before?"

Jupe dug into his pocket again and took out a second bit of gleaming metal. He handed it to the sheriff. "Because it was not there when Mr Thurgood bought the mine," said Jupiter. "When we were in the mine yesterday evening, I found this lodged in a wall, along with a number of other bits of metal. If you will examine it closely, you will see that it is greenish gold—probably gold with a high percentage of silver." Jupe rocked back on his heels.

"As we searched the hills for Pete and Allie last night, I started thinking about those two bits of gold. I knew that gold is often found alloyed with other metals—such as copper or silver—but I doubted that two completely different alloys would be found so close together. I also began to think about the shot we heard in the mine . . . and all the blasting. So I took a closer look at that bit of greenish gold. If you do that, Sheriff Tait, you will see that it was not always lodged in the wall of Death Trap Mine."

The sheriff held up the bit of metal and squinted at it. "It's . . . it's got a design on it!" he exclaimed.

Jupiter Jones nodded triumphantly. "A pattern of orange blossoms. That gold was once part of a wedding ring!"

Thurgood stepped forward. "Where did you get that?" he demanded. "Where did you really get it? And don't tell me you found it in the mine!"

"I don't need to tell you," said Jupe. "I'm sure that if you were careless enough to use pieces of old jewellery in your confidence game, there are other bits in the mine wall that can be identified. The sheriff has only to go and look at them."

He turned to the sheriff. "Mr Thurgood has been pulling a very old swindle," said Jupe. "He has been 'salting' his mine. He loaded a shotgun with bits of gold, fired the particles into the wall of the mine then brought in prospective investors to show them his 'strike'. He had his Mexican labourers set off dynamite whenever he brought in visitors, so that it would appear that the mine was actually being worked. I assume that the suckers flew to Lordsburg, where they were met by Thurgood. He then drove them to the Death Trap Mine and persuaded them to invest in the mine."

"Something doesn't make sense," Uncle Harry broke in. "Wesley Thurgood had already made a fortune in real estate. Why would he get involved in a crooked scheme like mine salting?"

Thurgood sneered. "That's simple. I wouldn't. The very idea is ridiculous."

"But when we go into the mine, we will see . . ." Jupe began.

"You will go nowhere!" shouted Thurgood. His face was now flushed and angry. His eyes darted to the entrance of the mine. "I am going to call my lawyer. In the meantime, anyone who sets foot in my mine had better have a search warrant, or they will be prosecuted."

"You can call your lawyer from jail," said Sheriff Tait. His eyes were cold. "I've got enough evidence to hold you on suspicion—and to get a search warrant."

"Are you going to believe that crazy kid?" cried Thurgood.

"He doesn't seem crazy to me," said the sheriff.

"Thank you, Sheriff Tait," said Jupe. "And now

there is one more thing I'd like to get cleared up."

He turned to Manny and Gasper.

"Where is Mrs Macomber?" demanded Jupiter. "Is she waiting to meet you somewhere?"

"Mrs Macomber?" said Manny, his face blank.

"The old dame who owns the houses across the way," Gasper explained. "Her name's Macomber."

A look of complete astonishment appeared on Jupe's face. "You mean . . . you mean you don't know her? You really don't know her?"

Manny shrugged.

Jupiter pulled hard at his bottom lip. "We suspected that Mrs Macomber was the fourth member of that Phoenix hold-up gang. But we had no real evidence to connect her with the robbery, except that she fits the description of the driver of the getaway car. She fits it perfectly. And she disappeared from Phoenix about the same time as the robbery. Then, after she learned we were investigating Morgan, she disappeared again."

Thurgood shouted, "I told you that kid was nuts. Who could ever suspect Mrs Macomber of being involved with those hoodlums!" Again Thurgood's eyes darted unconsciously to the entrance of the mine.

"If I'm nuts, why are you sweating, Thurgood?" demanded Jupe.

Suddenly Jupiter struck his forehead with the palm of his hand. "I'm an idiot!" he cried. "I thought Mrs Macomber disappeared because she was involved in that hold-up. But that wasn't it at all, was it, Thurgood? She disappeared because she knew *you!* She knew something about you that

147

you didn't want known. What happened to her, Thurgood? Where is Mrs Macomber?"

Thurgood swallowed. "How should I know?" He began to edge towards the mine. Jupe spun round, darted into the sheriff's car, and grabbed a powerful flashlight. He raced for the mine entrance.

The sheriff pointed at Thurgood. "Watch this man!" he roared to his deputy. Then he and Allie, Uncle Harry, Pete, and Bob followed Jupe into Death Trap Mine.

Jupe was well ahead, and the others stumbled after him as he sped down the mine tunnel and turned into the corridor that ran left. He passed the place where golden flecks showed briefly in the light.

Bob and Pete were close behind when Jupe ducked into the passageway that branched off to one side—the passageway that had led Allie to the dead thief. At the end of the tunnel, they stopped and looked down into the pit. There—tied and gagged but struggling mightily—was the missing lady.

20

Where's the Loot?

When mrs macomber saw the group above her, her eyes sparkled. Sheriff Tait quickly brought a ladder and climbed down into the pit after her.

"High time," she said as soon as he removed the gag. "I thought no one would ever come."

When she was untied, she calmly stood up, brushed herself off, and climbed up the ladder without help. The sheriff followed, carrying the suitcase that had been lying in the pit with her.

"Where is that scoundrel?" she demanded.

"Wesley Thurgood?" asked Jupe.

"He is *not* Wesley Thurgood!" said Mrs Macomber. "I finally remembered what was so unusual about that Thurgood baby. When he was born he had brown eyes. Hardly any babies are *born* with brown eyes. Most babies' eyes are blue, and if they're going to have brown eyes the colour changes after a while. But little Wesley Thurgood had brown eyes, and they don't change! That man's got blue eyes—he's an out-and-out impostor!"

"I suppose you told him that!" said Jupiter.

"Well, I asked him what he was up to. The next thing I knew, he was covering me with a shotgun. He made me get down in that hole and he threw my suitcase down after me. Where is he?"

"Outside," said the sheriff. "And he will shortly be in jail."

"Jail's too good for him!" declared Mrs Macomber.

"I agree, but it's the best we can do at the moment."

And, very shortly, the sheriff drove off with Wesley Thurgood as well as Manny and Gasper.

Sheriff Tait returned to the Christmas tree ranch late that afternoon. Uncle Harry and Magdalena had driven to Hambone to retrieve Mrs Macomber's truck. The widow herself sat in the Osborne living room having a cup of tea.

"Well?" she said, when she saw the sheriff.

The sheriff grinned at her, and at Allie and The Three Investigators. "You kids were right," he said. "Those two hoods confessed to the robbery of the armoured car five years ago. Not that it matters a lot. They're already wanted in four states for other stick-ups, and we'll charge them with kidnapping. Like you figured, Gilbert Morgan was one of the gang."

"But what about that rascal Thurgood?" demanded Mrs Macomber.

"He's waiting for a lawyer and he'll need one. We've got his fingerprints on the wire to Washington. My guess is that he's a professional con artist and he's probably got a record. They all do, no matter how slick they are. Of course he isn't Thurgood. I've been in touch with Los Angeles and I talked to the real Wesley Thurgood."

"I knew he was a phony from the beginning!"

crowed Allie. "You guys should have listened to me—especially after he lied and said that his antique car was used in *The Fortune Hunters*."

"Never mind about that," said Sheriff Tait. "I've got a search warrant and I'm going to go all through his place."

"You're looking for more evidence?" asked Bob.

"Yes, and I am looking for a quarter of a million dollars!" said the sheriff.

He paused to let this sink in, then went on. "According to Manny Ellis and Gasper—whose real name is Charlie Lambert—Gilbert Morgan and a woman named Hannah Troy were also involved in the Phoenix robbery. The woman drove the getaway car. She's in prison right now or she'd probably be here with Ellis and Lambert. They all went directly to Lordsburg and hid in a motel on the edge of town. But the next day Morgan gave them the slip and got away with the entire haul—$250,000! Ellis and Lambert never heard another thing about Morgan until his body turned up in the mine. They came, figuring the loot was still here, and I figure it's still here, too."

"But how do you know Thurgood didn't find it and stash it away somewhere?" asked Pete.

"That's not likely," answered Jupe. "If he found the money, why would he stay here and take the chances he took to pull off his mine swindle? Just consider it. After Morgan's body was found, the place was overrun with sightseers. Sheriff Tait was in and out. Yet Thurgood hired his Mexican labourers and brought in his investors and set off dynamite explosions in the mine. If I had found $250,000, I would simply have taken it and left."

"I would, too," said the sheriff. "That's why I figure the money is still up here someplace. The problem is, where? I know it's not in the mine because I searched all through there after Morgan's body was found. But maybe Morgan hid the loot in one of the old mine buildings—they were empty at the time."

"Hey, he could have put it in one of Mrs Macomber's houses," said Allie.

"Wow, let's start looking!" cried Pete. "A quarter of a million bucks!"

The group set to work right away. First they searched all of Mrs Macomber's houses. In one of them they found Harrison Osborne's missing machete hidden under a sofa, but there was no money. They pried into every corner of the cavernous old mine works and Thurgood's cabin. They combed through Wesley Thurgood's possessions. Although they found precise records of bank accounts and lists of names and addresses —probably of Thurgood's duped investors—they found nothing that would point to a hidden cache amounting to a quarter of a million dollars.

"There's one more chance." Jupe pointed across the fields to Uncle Harry's barn. "That's the only other building that was here five years ago when Gilbert Morgan came. Gasper tried to search it himself, but we scared him off. Morgan may have hidden the money someplace else, or buried it in the ground, but let's at least try the barn."

At first the barn seemed to offer few opportunities for a hiding place. The walls were simply wooden planks, held in place by uprights. The floor was hard bare earth, and the loft was empty except for dust and spiderwebs. Allie climbed into the old Model T and poked around without much enthusiasm. "Maybe Morgan didn't even have the money with him when he came to Twin Lakes," she said.

She sat down in the car, then looked surprised and wriggled slightly. "Seat's loose."

"Loose?" exclaimed Jupe. "Allie, get out."

"Migosh!" She leaped from the car.

Pete and Jupe quickly lifted the car seat and tumbled it into the back of the old auto.

"And there it is!" said Jupe triumphantly.

Sheriff Tait stepped to the car. In the space under the seat there were dozens of plastic-wrapped packages. The sheriff picked up one and opened it—and stared at a sheaf of twenty-dollar bills. They still looked new, crisp, and untouched.

"I wonder how long it takes to count to $250,000!" said Pete.

"I think it will take quite a while," said the sheriff. "I plan to count very slowly!"

21

A Souvenir for Mr Hitchcock

WHEN THE THREE INVESTIGATORS entered Alfred Hitchcock's office several days after their return to California, the famous motion-picture director regarded them with wry amusement. "On the telephone you announced that you had been in New Mexico pruning Christmas trees," he said. "Since you wished to see me as soon as possible, I assume that you managed to turn a prosaic summer job into an adventure among the evergreens."

Bob smiled and handed a file folder to the director.

"Aha!" said Mr Hitchcock, and he began to peruse the notes that Bob had made on the events connected with Death Trap Mine. When he finished reading he shot a reproachful look at Jupiter Jones.

"I trust that you are thoroughly ashamed of yourself," said Mr Hitchcock. "Entertaining such foul suspicions about Mrs Macomber! Where was the blameless widow, by the way, between the time she left that shop in Phoenix and the time she appeared in Twin Lakes? And where did she get the money to purchase her property?"

"She inherited the money," said Jupe. "She had an aged aunt who was suddenly taken ill and who sent for her. She left the shop without notice because the matter was extremely urgent, and also because she did not like the woman who owned the shop and didn't want to bother explaining things to her. Between May and September she was in El Paso nursing her aunt. The aunt died eventually— she was very old—leaving everything she owned to Mrs Macomber."

Mr Hitchcock nodded. "It is heartwarming when virtue is rewarded. Mrs Macomber sounds like a charming and rather unflappable woman. Certainly she recovered quickly after being imprisoned in that mine. I trust that the man who called himself Thurgood will be brought to justice?"

"On a number of counts," said Jupiter. "As the sheriff suspected, he is an experienced con man. His real name is John Manchester and he specializes in stock swindles. A number of his Death Trap Mine victims were wealthy men from Dallas. Manchester met them in a country club there, passed himself off as Thurgood, and convinced them that he had discovered a fabulously rich vein of gold in the old Death Trap Mine. He used forged documents to establish his false identity with Uncle Harry and a bank in Lordsburg, and he peddled forged stock certificates to the dupes who came to inspect his mine.

"Manchester's investment in the Death Trap Mine was small. He paid Harrison Osborne a thousand dollars down on the property and signed a note for twenty-five thousand dollars to be paid in instalments. He never intended to make any payments on that note. He was going to take the money he got from his victims, clean out his bank account, and disappear. That was his pattern; he had done it many times before."

Bob picked up the story from there. "But this time Mrs Macomber got in his way," he said. "After she accused Manchester of being a fake, he forced her into the pit and took her truck to Hambone. He abandoned it there and hiked back to Twin Lakes. He wanted people to think she had gone on vacation. That's why he packed her suitcase, too. We don't think he planned to leave her in the mine very long, or to hurt her. He just needed a little more time to finish his mine swindle. But things started happening so fast he never got a chance. Manny and Gasper saw to that!"

"What about the Mexicans?" asked Mr Hitchcock. "Surely they weren't in on the scheme."

"No, they weren't," Jupe replied. "Manchester needed workmen to make it look as if he were taking ore from the mine. He had them build the fence and start painting the house so everyone would think he was going to stay in Twin Lakes. The men were in this country illegally. So they were afraid to speak to anyone, and that's the way Manchester wanted it."

"Their story has a happy ending," said Bob. "Uncle Harry made arrangements with the authorities and they will remain in Twin Lakes legally and will prune his Christmas trees. And Magdalena has adopted the dog. She fed him until his sides bulged and now he's as tame as a puppy and he sleeps at the foot of her bed."

"I am delighted," said Mr Hitchcock. The motion-picture director leaned back in his desk chair. "A most interesting case," he mused. "How provoking that it will never be completely solved."

"What do you mean?" demanded Pete. "We solved it!"

"In all important respects, yes," replied Mr Hitchcock. "But I don't suppose anyone will ever know exactly what took place when Gilbert Morgan came to Twin Lakes five years ago, and why he hid the robbery proceeds in the old Ford."

"No," agreed Jupiter. "Morgan may have regarded the old car as a temporary hiding place for the money, then gone into the mine looking for a safer one. Was he still alive when the mine was sealed, or was he already dead? We will never know. Incidentally, we are quite sure Manchester found the body as soon as he opened the mine. He probably planned to blast that shaft closed—he wouldn't want to draw attention to himself by reporting the body. No wonder he was furious when he caught Allie in the Death Trap Mine.

"And since the Death Trap turned out to be such an unusual mine, we have brought you a souvenir of the place."

Jupe handed a small stone to the director, who took it and examined it with interest. "A nugget!" said Mr Hitchcock. "Thank you. I shall treasure it. Not everyone has a genuine gold nugget with orange blossoms engraved on it."

"Allie's got one," said Pete.

"I would say she deserves one," declared Mr Hitchcock.

"I guess so. She's an okay kid and she's got good instincts. I mean, she does kind of know about people. But she's so darned ... darned ..." said Pete.

"Energetic?" said Mr Hitchcock.

"You could say that." said Jupe. "You could also say she's about as comfortable to be with as—well, as a sockful of ants!"

From Alfred Hitchcock,
Master of Mystery and Suspense—

A thrilling series of detection and adventure. Meet The Three Investigators – Jupiter Jones, Peter Crenshaw and Bob Andrews. Their motto, "We Investigate Anything", leads the boys into some extraordinary situations – even Jupiter's formidable brain-power is sometimes stumped by the bizarre crimes and weird villains they encounter. But with the occasional piece of advice from The Master himself, The Three Investigators solve a whole lot of sensational mysteries.

1. The Secret of Terror Castle
2. The Mystery of the Stuttering Parrot
3. The Mystery of the Whispering Mummy
4. The Mystery of the Green Ghost
5. The Mystery of the Vanishing Treasure
6. The Secret of Skeleton Island
7. The Mystery of the Fiery Eye
8. The Mystery of the Silver Spider
9. The Mystery of the Screaming Clock
10. The Mystery of the Moaning Cave
11. The Mystery of the Talking Skull
12. The Mystery of the Laughing Shadow
13. The Secret of the Crooked Cat
14. The Mystery of the Coughing Dragon
15. The Mystery of the Flaming Footprints
16. The Mystery of the Nervous Lion
17. The Mystery of the Singing Serpent
18. The Mystery of the Shrinking House
19. The Secret of Phantom Lake
20. The Mystery of Monster Mountain
21. The Secret of the Haunted Mirror
22. The Mystery of the Dead Man's Riddle
23. The Mystery of the Invisible Dog

Armada

CAPTAIN ARMADA

has a whole shipload of exciting books for you

Here are just some of the best-selling titles that Armada has to offer:

- ⊐⊏ **The Clue of the Leaning Chimney** Carolyn Keene 65p
- ⊐⊏ **The Mystery of the Spiral Bridge** Franklin W. Dixon 65p
- ⊐⊏ **The Mystery of the Whispering Mummy** Alfred Hitchcock 65p
- ⊐⊏ **The Mystery of the Stuttering Parrot** Alfred Hitchcock 60p
- ⊐⊏ **The Ring O'Bells Mystery** Enid Blyton 65p
- ⊐⊏ **The Secret of the Old Mill** Franklin W. Dixon 65p
- ⊐⊏ **The Moon Raiders** Patrick Moore 50p
- ⊐⊏ **Bailey's Bird** Geoffrey Morgan 50p
- ⊐⊏ **Biggles Hunts Big Game** Capt. W. E. Johns 60p
- ⊐⊏ **Lone Pine London** Malcolm Saville 60p

Armadas are available in bookshops and newsagents, but can also be ordered by post.

HOW TO ORDER

ARMADA BOOKS, Cash Sales Dept., GPO Box 29, Douglas, Isle of Man, British Isles. Please send purchase price of book plus postage, as follows:—

    1—4 Books .... 8p per copy
    5 Books or more .... no further charge
    25 Books sent post free within U.K.

Overseas Customers

    1 Book: 10p. Additional books 5p per copy

NAME (Block letters)

_____

ADDRESS

_____

_____

_____

While every effort is made to keep prices low, it is sometimes necessary to increase prices on short notice. Armada Books reserve the right to show new retail prices on covers which may differ from those previously advertised in the text or elsewhere.